PRINCESS FROM THE SHADOWS

Maisey Yates

MILLS &
BOON

First published in Great Britain 2012
by Mills & Boon, an imprint of Harlequin (UK) Limited,
Large Print edition 2012
Harlequin (UK) Limited,
Eton House, 18-24 Paradise Road, Richmond, Surrey TW9 1SR

© Harlequin Books S.A. 2012

Special thanks and acknowledgement are given to Maisey Yates for her contribution to *The Santina Crown* series.

ISBN: 978 0 263 23727 6

Harlequin (UK) policy is to use papers that are natural, renewable and recyclable products and made from wood grown in sustainable forests. The logging and manufacturing process conform to the legal environmental regulations of the country of origin.

Printed and bound in Great Britain
by CPI Antony Rowe, Chippenham, Wiltshire

THE SANTINA CROWN

Royalty has never been so scandalous!

STOP PRESS—
Crown Prince in shock marriage

The tabloid headlines…

When HRH Crown Prince Alessandro of Santina proposes to paparazzi favourite Allegra Jackson it promises to be *the* social event of the decade— outrageous headlines guaranteed!

The salacious gossip…

Mills & Boon invites you to rub shoulders with royalty, sheikhs and glamorous socialites. Step into the decadent playground of the world's rich and famous…

THE SANTINA CROWN

THE PRICE OF ROYAL DUTY
Penny Jordan

THE SHEIKH'S HEIR
Sharon Kendrick

THE SCANDALOUS PRINCESS
Kate Hewitt

THE MAN BEHIND THE SCARS
Caitlin Crews

DEFYING THE PRINCE
Sarah Morgan

PRINCESS FROM THE SHADOWS
Maisey Yates

THE GIRL NOBODY WANTED
Lynn Raye Harris

PLAYING THE ROYAL GAME
Carol Marinelli

MAISEY YATES

was an avid Mills & Boon® Modern™ Romance reader before she began to write them. She still can't quite believe she's lucky enough to get to create her very own sexy alpha heroes and feisty heroines. Seeing her name on one of those lovely covers is a dream come true.

Maisey lives with her handsome, wonderful, diaper-changing husband and three small children across the street from her extremely supportive parents and the home she grew up in, in the wilds of Southern Oregon, USA. She enjoys the contrast of living in a place where you might wake up to find a bear on your back porch and then heading into the home office to write stories that take place in exotic urban locales.

CHAPTER ONE

"WHAT do you mean she's gone?" Prince Rodriguez Anguiano looked down at Eduardo Santina, King of Santina, and his future father-in-law, and swore he saw sweat beading on the older man's brow.

The king was known for being formidable, tough and unbending. Watching him sweat was unexpected. And more than a little bit interesting.

King Eduardo cleared his throat. "Just that. Sophia is gone. She left with a maharaja."

Rodriguez felt a smile tug at the corner of his mouth. "A maharaja? Is marrying a prince not enough for some women? They feel the need to pursue a more…exotic title?"

King Eduardo's face darkened, color creeping into his cheeks. "She has done so without my permission."

"I'm assuming, since my intended fiancée has run away with a maharaja, the wedding is off?" The king only looked at him and Rodriguez felt a vague sense of relief wash through him. He had been prepared to do the marriage thing, but truly, he hadn't been looking forward to it. In his estimation it was a ball and chain situation, and he didn't know anyone who would willingly shackle themselves in that manner. Yet people did seem to get married. It was the heir factor, one he couldn't ignore forever, but for a while longer, maybe.

Sophia had been pretty enough, a beautiful brunette with a real classic beauty. But even that would get old after a while. Now he could go back to Santa Christobel and celebrate with a blonde. Maybe a redhead. Maybe both. Not that he usually went in for that sort of thing but he'd had six long, unheard-of months of celibacy so that he could present his future bride with medical proof of his good health. And now that there would be no wedding, it had just been six months of physical torture.

"Father?"

Rodriguez turned, his ears always tuned in to sultry, feminine tones. But in this instance, the tone did not match the looks. One of Eduardo's other daughters was standing in the entryway, sleek brown hair hanging just beneath her chin.

All no-nonsense and practical, as was the rest of her attire.

Wide-leg beige slacks, a white button-up top and metallic ballet slipper-style shoes. She looked like she'd stepped out of the pages of a business-casual catalog. She was tall, slim, only a couple of inches shorter than he was, and her face was pleasant enough, but with none of the flash and paint he was accustomed to seeing on a woman.

"Sorry," she said, inclining her head. "I didn't realize that you were busy." She turned to go, and for some reason, he was sorry to see it.

"Carlotta."

She paused and turned back again. This time he noticed how green her eyes were. "Yes, Father?"

"Stay for a moment."

Carlotta gave him a brief icy look before turning her focus back to her father.

"This is Prince Rodriguez Anguiano. Your sister Sophia's fiancé."

She looked at him again, her expression blank. She was strange, contained, demure almost, and yet he could sense something beneath it. Something she seemed determined not to reveal.

"Charmed," he said, flashing her a grin. "Though

I don't know that I'm Sophia's fiancé any longer. As she's run off with the maharaja."

Carlotta blinked owlish green eyes at him before shooting her father a worried look. That's where her emotion was, reserved for the old man. She seemed to fear him, or at least feel nervous around him. Rodriguez couldn't even find the slightest bit of fear in himself. The king posed no threat to him. A lion who was all roar and no maul. He knew the other kind, the kind who wouldn't hesitate to tear out your throat. It made it very hard to take a man like Eduardo Santina seriously.

His daughter, on the other hand, seemed to feel differently.

"She did not 'run off' with the mahar—with Ashok," Eduardo said.

"I don't care if she walked, ran or flew in his private jet. The bottom line is the same. I am out a fiancée, and we seem to have no more marriage bargain," Rodriguez countered.

Carlotta shifted on her sensible shoes. "Can I go?"

"No," her father said.

"I don't really care what you do," Rodriguez threw in, mildly amused by the whole situation.

What adult woman asked her father for permission to do anything? Obviously not his ex–intended bride, Sophia Santina. But apparently Carlotta Santina was another matter.

Carlotta's eyes narrowed slightly in his direction, before flickering back to her father. "I need to call Luca before…"

"It can wait, Carlotta. Do me this one favor," Eduardo bit out roughly, the strain of the situation not well hidden.

Carlotta seemed to shrink and Rodriguez felt his stomach turn sour. *Dios*, but he hated men like that. Men who used their strength, their power, over others like that. Over their own children.

"I'm done here, actually," Rodriguez said. "If you have no bride for me, I have no reason to stay." *Unless one of the maids is looking to get lucky.*

"Tell me, Rodriguez, did you have feelings for Sophia?" Eduardo asked.

"You know I didn't. I didn't even know her. I won't insult either of us by pretending otherwise."

"Then it was her name you needed? Not her?"

He couldn't care less who he married so long as

she could produce heirs and do a nice royal wave from a balcony. "You know that to be true."

"Then I do have a bride for you." Eduardo turned his dark eyes on Carlotta. "You can have Carlotta."

Carlotta blinked hard and looked from Rodriguez back to her father. She was certain her ears couldn't be working right, because she had thought she'd heard her father give her away. Like she was a thing. A parting gift for the visiting prince.

Are you shocked? He already believes you gave yourself away.

She shook the thought off and continued to stare at her father, letting the silence fill the room until it became oppressive.

Finally, Rodriguez laughed, a short, harsh sound. "A trade?"

"A way to keep our bargain, Prince Rodriguez."

Carlotta shook her head, and she knew her eyes were probably comically large in her head. She closed her mouth. She hadn't realized it had dropped open.

She'd been completely floored by her sister,

sweet Sophia, running away from her arranged marriage to Rodriguez, especially as it was so important for Santina and Santa Christobel to forge an alliance. She'd been the first to warn her sister about the unflattering headlines. *Princess Sophia Joins Mile-High Club.*

But she hadn't realized that she would get dragged into the whole debacle. And certainly not to this degree.

Rodriguez flicked her a dismissive glance. "I have no interest in taking a wife who nearly faints at the thought of becoming my bride. I'm certain I can find someone my mere presence does not offend. We have no deal, Eduardo."

He turned and walked out of the room, leaving Carlotta alone with her father. It was a new kind of silence that filled the room now. One bursting with rage, combined with a kind of leaden disappointment that she could feel down in her soul, weighting her, climbing in her throat, threatening to strangle her.

She knew this feeling. Had felt it before. In this very room. In this very spot.

Nearly six years ago she'd been here. In her father's office. Her knees locked, her feet glued to the carpet, hands clasped tightly in front of her. Her entire body shaking, a cold sweat covering her back, her neck.

I'm pregnant.

They had been the two most terrifying words she'd ever spoken in her life. And directly after them had come the most sickening minute of silence she'd ever endured.

Until now.

"Father, I…"

"Carlotta, after all I have done for you," he said, his voice thick with disappointment, "you cannot do this for me? For your country? You brought so much shame upon us, all of us. The people of Santina, your family."

"I…I only came in to tell you that I have to return tonight." She couldn't deal with her father's words. They hurt too badly. They rang too true. "Luca needs me and…and then you throw a prince at me! A marriage proposal. I don't…" She swallowed, trying to suppress the panic that was starting to rise in her. "What do you expect of me?"

Her father looked down at his hands, folded in front of him on his neat, expansive desk. "I had hoped that you would understand how important this was. I had hoped you would understand your duty. After all our family has endured recently in the press, thanks to your brother. After the way they publicized your shame."

Carlotta felt her face grow tense, needles of icy cold rage dotting her cheeks. Luca wasn't her shame. And he never could be. Even if the press had been determined to make him so.

The Sole Santina Bastard. A favored headline at the time of Luca's birth. She could only thank God they didn't know the whole story. That they didn't know the half of the sins she was capable of committing when she let the hold on her control loosen.

And Father is the only reason they don't.

That brought the guilt. Right on time.

"I have always believed that you would do great things, Carlotta," he said, his voice softer now. "This is your chance to prove me right." He looked up at her, his dark eyes shining, and she felt her stomach tighten. "You are my most beloved daughter. I did everything in my power to protect you, to keep the press from finding out the details surrounding Luca's birth. Is it so much to ask for this?"

She felt like she was choking, as if her throat was getting tighter with each word her father spoke. Yet another reason she avoided Santina. Her family. The obligations of being a princess. The horrible, crushing guilt.

Not for the first time, she felt like coming home had been a mistake. She didn't know where she fit anymore. She'd been on the fringes of the glamorous engagement party, not entirely able to join in with her family. Not able to join in with her brother Alessandro's new in-laws, the Jacksons, and their carefree, crass style of behavior. In a way she almost envied the Jacksons. They didn't have to worry about how they were perceived. They didn't seem to worry about anything.

Yes, but you do.

It was easier when she was in her home on the Amalfi Coast. When she was just Carlotta, Luca's mum.

But that was a dream. A dream she'd escaped to when she'd been pregnant, alone and scared. Heartbroken. Hounded by the press.

She'd been weak then. But she could never have

come out of it remaining weak. It was either grow a spine or melt into a puddle and die. And for Luca's sake, melting had never been a viable option. She'd had to find inner strength, and she'd found it quickly.

Still, facing down her father brought back the girl she'd been. The one who had wanted to please him so badly. Who had only wanted to do right. With everything that was going on, Sophia's very public fall from grace, Alex's marriage…maybe it was her chance to grab a little redemption. To be the daughter her father seemed to believe she still could be.

"What is the precise nature of your agreement with…with Prince Rodriguez?" she asked, licking her suddenly dry lips.

"Anguiano needs an heir," said Eduardo. "His father is dying. As good as dead. Incapacitated and in hospital. It's time for Rodriguez to take the throne of Santa Christobel, and that means he needs a wife."

"And what's in it for us? For Santina. I mean, I understand it in a general sense. But if I'm actually going to…marry Prince Rodriguez, then I need to know exactly what we stand to gain."

"Can you imagine it, Carlotta? What such an alliance could bring? Ease for educational programs between the nations. Trade. A valuable ally to stand with should conflict ever arise. All cemented by marriage. Children. It is unfathomable in its value."

"Gems," she said softly, a realization washing over her. "They have diamonds. Ruby mines too. A host of other natural resources."

"It cannot be overlooked. They are a wealthy nation. And that makes them even more valuable. Sophia knew her duty. She has abandoned it. But I trust you, Carlotta. I trust that you will do what is right."

What *was* right? She had tried to do what was right for most of her life. Barring one giant mistake, she always had. It had always been her goal. To be the kind of daughter her parents deserved and desired. She didn't know if she could take it this far though.

She closed her eyes for a moment, pictured her house on the beach. The quiet. Her son running through the halls with his arms full of stuffed animals that had most definitely seen better days. Things were simpler there. She didn't have to work so hard to be the Carlotta that she was expected to be. The one she feared deep inside she never truly could be.

But while she had left palace life behind, she hadn't left her title. She hadn't truly shed her duty.

That was bred into her. A part of her. Even if she tried to ignore it.

And then, there was her father. Who had never given up on her. Not even when she'd let him down, dragged the Santina name through the mud. Put them on par with the kind of tabloid fodder he despised.

For all the cruel words her family had bandied around about her older brother Alessandro's future in-laws, the very same could be said about her. It *had* been said about her, in bold print, on newsstands all around Santina.

Scandalous. Immoral.

Her family, her father, had never thrown those words at her, but she knew it had been thought. How could they not think it? She had. Worse, she knew it was true. A lifetime of keeping her passionate, exuberant nature on a tight leash, and in one great fall from grace, all her efforts had been reduced to nothing. She had tainted her family name, had brought them ridicule, the disgust of a nation who saw her as a clear sign of the degeneration of the royal family.

The question was, how badly did she want redemption? Enough to marry a total stranger? The prince of a country she'd never been to? The man her sister had been engaged to, until she'd broken it by hooking up with Ash on his private plane.

She looked at her father. He had aged in the past few years. She hadn't been around to see it. She wondered how much of it was her fault. How many lines on his face were from dealing with her transgressions.

It made her sick to think of it.

But she could be the one to fix things here. The one to save the day. To be the daughter her parents had imagined she would be. It was almost embarrassing that she wanted it so badly. That she cared so much. But she did. She needed to look at her father and see something other than disappointment in his eyes.

"What do you need me to do?" she asked.

Rodriguez reclined on the bed, his shoes consigned to the floor, along with his tie. His plane would be ready soon, and then he would be leaving Santina, and with it, the little melodrama that the Santinas seemed to be living.

He didn't waste his time on this sort of thing. He lived. He didn't regret. He didn't worry. He didn't think more than he had to. Not about anything beyond the here and now anyway.

There was a soft knock at the door and he wondered if it was a maid, then chuckled at where the thought took him. It really had been too long since he'd had sex. He'd been expecting to pick up a fiancée so he'd imagined his celibacy wouldn't have lasted beyond tonight.

"Sì?"

The door opened, and it wasn't a maid. It was Princess Carlotta Santina, still in her drab outfit, her lips pursed tight. She didn't look like she was here to alleviate him of his celibacy either.

"I thought we might have a talk." No, definitely not.

"Did you?"

She nodded, the setting sun filtering through the window shimmering over her straight, glossy bob. "I thought, since my father just tried to…use me as a stand-in for my sister, we might…"

"I'm actually done with that now." He really wasn't in the mood for whatever kind of rant she'd come to throw at him. Or was she here to apologize? The way she'd looked at her father, the way her shoulders had folded in, her hands clasped tight in front of her, almost like a shield. Like she feared him...she would come and apologize.

"I'm not," she said, the slight steel in her tone surprising him.

"Is that so?"

"Yes. My father explained the situation to me more fully. I...I knew that you and Sophia were engaged, in a sense, but I did not know the specifics. I don't live in Santina so I'm not really in on everything that goes on here and Sophia didn't... she didn't really say much of anything about you. I only got wind of how big of a deal it was when the story broke about Sophia being caught with Ash on the plane."

"That's because I've barely met the girl. No reason for her to talk about me."

Carlotta cleared her throat. "Yes, well...*the girl*, is gone."

"With the maharaja."

He saw the corner of her mouth twitch. "Right.

With Ash. Alex's friend. And you still need a wife."

"Need is a strong word."

"Do you or don't you?" she asked.

"Eventually."

"How soon is this *eventually* you speak of?"

"Truthfully? The sooner, the better. This will be a time of transition for my people." He thought of the responsibility, the weight of the crown. It was heavy on his shoulders. Already he'd moved back into the palace in Santa Christobel. He felt like it would choke him, being inside those four walls again. "Anything that can be done to ease their fears at this time would be welcome. Marriage, my marriage, would help with that."

They wouldn't be mourning his father, that was for sure. Carlos Anguiano was not much loved. And while Rodriguez had essentially been running Santa Christobel for the past several years, his father had remained the figurehead.

"It would mean a new start for my people. A fresh beginning," he said.

"Well then, I guess I have good news for you."

"What is that?"

"I haven't run off with a maharaja, so…I happen to be available to marry you. At your earliest convenience."

It was a rare moment that found Rodriguez Anguiano speechless.

"Excuse me?" he asked.

"I'll marry you."

"What happened to the emphatic no from earlier?"

"I was shocked. In shock. I wasn't prepared for something like that."

"To be offered up as a replacement wife in your sister's absence?" He sat up and swung his legs over the side of the bed, standing quickly.

"I wasn't...exactly expecting that, no. I thought I'd come to the party, have a couple of drinks and go home. Wasn't really anticipating acquiring a husband."

"And yet you have changed your mind?" he asked, pacing in front of her, adrenaline surging through him, joining the unrest he'd already felt being contained in the walls of the castle in Santina. That he'd been feeling since he'd boarded his private plane, on his way to collect what could only be described as a ball and chain.

"We need this, don't we? The marriage I..." He

watched her throat convulse as she swallowed. "I have always known that I would face an arranged marriage of some kind."

She spoke the truth. From the cradle they'd all known their marriages would likely be arranged by their parents. Because duty came first, the allegiance to the family name. To Santina. Alex had long been promised to Anna, a woman more than suitable to be the future queen of Santina. But that was before he'd gone rogue and set his sights on Allegra Jackson. And of course Sophia had been promised to Rodriguez. Natalia's engagement was in the process of being arranged. She didn't know about Matteo, but it was less urgent now that Alex was formally betrothed.

Before Carlotta had... Well, if not for Luca her father would have likely arranged a marriage for her years ago. As it was, she had been sort of taken out of the "dynastic union" running when she'd had her son.

Well, apparently not really out of the running. She was good enough to play second string. Good enough to marry the renowned rebel prince of Santa Christobel. A man who lived dangerously and loved often. Well, not *loved*. He made love often, according to the tabloids. A new woman on his arm every weekend to accompany him to Europe's most exclusive parties. Fast cars, fast dates.

The kind of man who represented recklessness, lawlessness, total disregard for honor. A man who served his own passions. The kind of man she hated. The kind of man she was so easily drawn to.

"As have I," Rodriguez said, his dark eyes unreadable, the little curve of his mouth still present, like it had been earlier. It was a kind of ever-present near-smile that made it look like he was mocking her. It made her stomach feel like it was being squeezed tight by an invisible fist.

She cleared her throat. "So, while I hadn't really penciled a wedding into my day planner, it's not a…it's not a total surprise."

What was her other option anyway?

Well, there was staying in Italy. That was a good thought. Hiding. But she didn't know if it served any real purpose. The only person it really helped was her. It allowed her to lick her wounds in private. It allowed her to hide Luca from royal life. Something part of her wanted to do, but something she also knew wasn't fair. He was a Santina. He was a royal. It was a part of him, and it didn't do him any good to force him to deny that part of himself. No matter how much simpler it would be to just raise him as an ordinary little boy. Who wasn't tabloid fodder. It wasn't reality.

"I don't suppose you really had other life plans either," she said.

"I don't plan. I live."

"Well…I suppose that means you don't have a woman back home you're dying to see. Someone you'd prefer to marry."

"I'll be honest with you, Carlotta, I prefer not to marry. But I need an heir. One that isn't a bastard."

She flinched when he spoke the word. She hated that word. One used to label an innocent child, to make them suffer for the perceived sins of his parents. Did Rodriguez know about Luca? He had to know. So, he'd chosen the words to wound her.

"Why?" she said. "Do you have many? Children, I mean."

"Me? No. I always use protection." Such a throwaway statement. Spoken like a man who never thought about anyone but himself.

She gritted her teeth. "It doesn't always work."

"True. But in the event that a pregnancy had resulted, you can bet the woman involved would have told me. I'm rich. Titled. She would have wanted her piece."

"You would have owed her a piece," she said. "At minimum."

"I'm not arguing that. My point is that, whether I want marriage or not, I need it."

"Preferably to me."

He looked at her, his dark gaze dismissive. "Because of connection to this family."

"I didn't seek to imply otherwise. It's the only reason I would marry you."

"Because your father told you to. That's the reason."

She felt her cheeks heat. "He has good reasons."

"Fine. But you're still doing it because he asked you to."

"And your father has nothing to do with any of this?"

A muscle in his jaw ticked, the light in his eyes turning black, deadly. "My father can hardly lift his hand anymore. He is weak. What I do, I do for my country."

"Same goes for me. But my family *is* Santina."

"Thank goodness mine is not Santa Christobel. Santa Christobel is better than the Anguiano legacy has been thus far. But I intend to do better."

"And I intend to…be a part of it." It was strange, lobbying for something she wasn't certain she wanted. But she needed it. Everything else aside, her father was right. She had made mistakes that had cost the family. And he had covered for her. Had done everything in his power to keep her from being utterly humiliated and exposed.

In the scope of things, this wasn't so very much to ask.

"Does it get boring?"

"What?" she asked, trying to ignore the glint of humor in his dark eyes. It made him seem… attractive. Well, he was attractive, glint or no, with his golden skin and dark hair that was much too long to be considered respectable for a man of his station. Chiseled jaw, a body that looked as though it would be hard like iron. It wouldn't be impersonal or cold like metal, though. No, he would be hot.…

She blinked, trying to reroute her thoughts. She didn't do the man thing. Not anymore. Just acknowledging the speed and ease with which he aroused her was…horrifying. Even more horrifying was the strength of it. Why was it so hard to be good? To be the woman she was supposed to be?

"Being this noble, does it get boring?"

"Yes. It does. Which is why I practice it in small doses." And throw it off altogether sometimes…

"Good to know that not even you are always respectable."

"Not even close." But she tried. She'd tried all her life. To ignore the fire that seemed to burn so close to the surface of her skin. To be the demure princess she was expected to be. It had been a battle all her life. One she'd lost completely when she'd met Luca's father. A lifetime of practiced restraint reduced to nothing in just a few short weeks.

He inclined his head. "All right then, Princess Carlotta, you have yourself a marriage bargain. My plane leaves Santina late tonight and I intend to take my future wife with me."

"I…I can't leave from here. I can't leave tonight." Luca was still in Italy, with his nanny. So were all of her things. Her real things, not her princess trappings.

"Why is that?"

"Because I don't live here at the palace. I don't even live on the island. I live in Italy. My home is there, my...everything." She didn't know what stopped her from saying something about Luca. Maybe because he hadn't mentioned him. The whole thing seemed so mercenary. So cold. Adding him to it...it just seemed wrong.

"Fine. We'll stop in Italy on our way to Santa Christobel."

Oh, yes, and pick up her five-year-old with Mr. Tall, Dark, Sexy and Imposing standing in the doorway with that mocking grin of his. No thank you.

"I can make my own way to Santa Christobel," she said archly. "I need time to prepare."

"Have a lover you need to cast off before we get married?"

She nearly snorted. She'd lived the past few years completely abstinent after only one, near emotionally fatal affair. "Oh, yes, a stable of them. You?"

"I don't intend to cast anyone off."

"Excuse me?"

He shrugged. "I don't intend to cast off any lovers just because I'm getting married."

Her stomach twisted. Men. They really were all the same. Cheating, lying jerks who only cared about pleasing their sex drives. "I hope you don't think you'll be in my bed then. I don't share."

A slow smile spread over his handsome face, teeth bright white against his tan skin. "I do."

"What does that mean?"

"It means I don't ask for what I don't give."

"Fidelity?"

"Exactly."

"Well, I ask for fidelity." *I've never gotten it, but I'd like it.* "And if you're going to be in my bed, you won't be in anyone else's." She couldn't believe she was even talking about beds and sex with a man she'd only just meant.

It was making her face hot, and not, she suspected, from embarrassment. From that nearly six years of celibacy maybe. From the thought of a man's hands, *his* hands, on her skin again. Kissing. Caressing.

She shifted and tried to ease the knot in her

stomach with a deep breath. That was one part of marriage that wouldn't be so bad.

Unless he's actively sleeping with other women the whole time.

Yeah, that was a definite no-go for her. And anyway, contemplating sleeping with him was… he was a stranger and it was bad with a capital *B*.

"We will discuss this no more. Not now."

She raised her brow. "Excuse me?"

"It is immaterial. Fine details you and I will work out later. For now, the real question is, will you marry me?"

He didn't get down on one knee or anything, thank goodness, because that would have been just too much. He stood in front of her, arms crossed over his broad chest, a knowing smile curving his lips. He exuded confidence. Charm. That kind of cocky, arrogant sexiness that said he knew just what he could make a woman feel.

He wasn't the first man she'd met who exuded those things.

He took a step toward her, his dark eyes trained on hers, and for a moment, it felt like the world had closed in on them. So that it was just the two of them.

Rodriguez didn't touch her, he didn't even make a move to touch her, and yet she felt like he had. Could feel the warmth coming from his hard body and she wasn't afraid of him putting his hands on her, she was wishing he would. Aching for it.

"A simple question, a simple answer," he said. "Yes or no?"

She met his dark gaze, her heart hopping in her chest like a caged bird making a bid for freedom. She opened her mouth to speak but her throat was dry. She swallowed, trying to find her balance, her confidence.

Trying to find the woman that knew all about men like him, who knew that charm was nothing more than smoke and mirrors; that sex, no matter how fulfilling or meaningful she might find it, was nothing more than a little bit of amusement for men like him, and that they would leave the woman to pick up the check. A week's worth of fun for them, could mean a lifetime of payment for the woman involved.

It had for her.

And she would never be that stupid again. She would never again buy into the kind of sweet lies that could be issued from wicked, sexy mouths like his. Not even if she was married to the charmer.

Married. Was she really going to marry him? Could she really go back to her father and tell him she'd decided not to?

"Yes," she said, the word weak, breathless. She cleared her throat. She didn't do weak and breathless. Not anymore. She'd made the decision, she would stand strong in it. "Yes, I will marry you."

CHAPTER TWO

HE WAS a small boy. He barely came to the top of Carlotta's hip. Dark hair, the same green eyes as his mother.

His mother. Carlotta.

Dios.

He knew it, the moment he saw her bend and help the little boy from the back of the limo when they'd pulled up to the palace, knew from the moment he saw the boy's face. That same sullen expression, the stubborn chin, he was hers.

He had inherited a child, along with a fiancée.

Part of him knew it shouldn't matter. That it didn't truly change anything. He and Carlotta had been planning on having children. He needed an heir after all. That he would be a father one day was, and had always been, a given.

Another part of him felt a kind of bone-deep terror that had been absent from him since he was a boy himself. He remembered that day, the day when his emotions had finally given beneath the strain of living a life beneath his father's iron fist. The day his emotions had deserted him entirely.

Well, that fear he'd thought long gone was here now. Because of the boy. Reflected in the boy. He was afraid, his eyes wide on the castle in front of him. It couldn't be his first time seeing a palace. His grandmother and grandfather were the rulers of Santina. He *was* a Santina.

Carlotta looked at him, her green eyes hard. "Hello."

"Hola," he said.

"Hi." This from the boy.

Rodriguez looked down at him, swallowing, trying to bring some moisture to his suddenly dry throat. It seemed like the right thing to introduce himself to the boy. Did you introduce yourself formally to a child?

Annoyance mixed with uncertainty. Carlotta had managed to catch him off guard twice now. They were the only two times it had happened in his recent memory. This wasn't a trend he liked.

He would just approach the chiild as he would an adult. "I am Prince Rodriguez Anguiano. What is your name?" That earned him little more than a wide-eyed stare from those green eyes.

"Luca," said Carlotta. "His name is Luca."

That she answered annoyed him, like she didn't want her son speaking to him. It also made him feel a small measure of relief. Because it spared him from having to talk directly to Luca.

"Come with me," he said, turning and heading to the palace.

He nearly laughed. He had been pretending that marrying Carlotta rather than Sophia changed nothing. And had been managing quite well. But now there was this…complication.

This was a difference that would be hard to ignore.

The massive doors to the palace opened and he ushered them in to the cavernous entryway. All glossy marble with a domed ceiling depicting intricate scenes of men and angels. Not to his taste at all. He'd never felt at home here. There was a reason he'd spent his young adult years in France and Spain, a reason he had his own penthouse in Barcelona still, even though his time avoiding Santa Christobel was over.

But now that his father was in the hospital, now

that running the country was up to him, he'd had no choice but to come back. Even though it made him feel like he'd crawled into someone else's skin. Ill-fitting. Uncomfortable. Nearly unbearable.

Now, another role he wasn't made for. Husband. Father.

"There is no…no room prepared for Luca," he said, careful not to look down at the top of the boy's dark head.

"What?" she asked, finely arched brows locking together.

He gritted his teeth against rising annoyance. "Had you told me there would be a need…"

"You didn't know?" She shot a look to Luca, then back to him, her eyes round with shock. "How did you not know?"

Luca was watching both of them, confusion in his eyes. That was something he remembered well about being a child. That lack of control. Knowing that your fate was in the hands of the adults around you. How little sense it made sometimes.

His stomach tightened, and he looked down at

the boy again. "Luca, perhaps you would like to come out to the garden?"

The garden. Such as it was. It was a massive, sprawling green field in comparison to most lawns. But it was likely to keep a child busy. At least, he thought it would.

Luca nodded. "I like to play outside. Do you have a slide?"

Rodriguez looked at Carlotta, then back at Luca, a strange sensation—nerves?—making it hard to breathe. "No. No slides. But we could put one in." Put one in? Like they were staying?

Of course they were staying. He'd signed a new marriage contract with King Eduardo before leaving Santina. But he hadn't known about the child. About Luca. He'd known that he and Carlotta would have an heir…but an heir was… It sounded very detached. Unreal. The little boy with serious green eyes was real.

Too real.

"You don't have to put a slide in," said Carlotta. "Well, not today. Eventually I guess it might… Luca, let's go outside." She held out her hand and Luca wrapped his small fingers around hers. She looked at Rodriguez and he nodded, leading her through the entryway and down the main corridor that led out to the back terrace.

They stepped outside into the warm evening, the heat of the day long past, the setting sun casting electric orange stripes over the vivid green lawn.

"There isn't a pond or anything is there?" she asked, eyeing the fenced-in area.

"No. It's safe for him. This part here is just grass."

"Go, run," she said.

Luca smiled at Carlotta and trotted off the terrace, and Carlotta watched him, a soft expression on her face.

"The plane ride was long," she said. "He really needed to get out and move."

"I can imagine." He'd learned not to fidget from a very early age. It had stayed with him into adulthood. Sometimes, even now, if he was in a meeting and he found himself fidgeting, he could still imagine that the sharp crack of a ruler on his shins might come next.

"How did you not know?" she asked.

"About Luca? How was I supposed to know?"

"It was… The press, they… He's the only illegitimate Santina. The headlines were not kind."

"I don't read tabloids."

"You don't?"

"No."

"Not even when they're talking about you?"

"Especially not then," he said.

"How do you…I mean, how can you not? I had to…I had to know what they were saying." She looked away from him, her eyes on Luca, who was now turning circles in the middle of the large expanse of grass. "I suppose, looking back, it wasn't the healthiest thing for a hormonal, pregnant woman to do. But I just felt like I needed to know."

"I don't care what they're saying. Anyway, what they write about me is simply a rundown of my weekend's events. If I want a recap, I'll look at the pictures I took."

She turned her head sharply, her eyes wide. "Pictures?"

"Oh, so you've read about me then," he said.

"I said I read tabloids. Anyway, who hasn't read about you?"

"Probably a few priests who are trying to deny the existence of evil in the world, but we aren't supposed to be talking about me right now. I didn't know you had a son."

"Does it change anything?"

Did it? He'd never planned on being very involved with his wife and children. He just…he couldn't think of a single thing he could add to their lives. They would serve their purpose, likely better without his interference. He knew nothing about family. The only thing he knew about children was what not to do with them.

That was something, he supposed.

"I don't know that it does," he said. "Is his father in the picture?"

"Luca doesn't have a father." Carlotta felt her cheeks get hot as Rodriguez fixed her with a hard stare. "Well…obviously he has a father," she said. "But he doesn't have an involved father."

"Messy breakup?" he asked.

It suddenly seemed a bit harder to breathe. "You could say that." It would be an understatement, but she wasn't in the mood to elaborate.

"So I'm not going to get tangled up in any sort of custody thing?"

"Absolutely not. Is that your only concern?"

"I don't see anything else that should concern me."

"You don't see how having a son concerns you?"

His eyebrows locked together. "He's not my son."

Carlotta's heart twisted tight. It was a fair enough statement. Luca wasn't Rodriguez's son. And they'd been at his home for all of fifteen minutes. He wasn't being cruel. Still, it felt a little cruel. "No, I know. But he is a child, and if you're going to be my husband he will be your stepson, and that means some of the responsibility…"

"He has a nanny?"

"Yes. She had to stay behind for a couple of days but…"

"In that case, I see my responsibility will be limited."

Anger burned in her, threatening to swallow her whole. "And will it be the same for *your* children? Because if not, you and I have no more to say to each other. Luca is my son. He's my world and if you—"

"Yes. It will be the same for our *child*. I don't intend to have any more than is required."

"If we have a girl?"

"Then we will have to have more, I suppose."

"I don't…I don't even know how to have this discussion with you," she said, panic clawing at her stomach. How could she stand here talking children with this stranger? Was she really going to marry this man?

Yes. Because the other option was going back to her father, standing in that spot in his office and telling him, yet again, how badly she'd failed the Santina family. She couldn't do it. The guilt would consume her. She lived with enough guilt. No sense in adding to it.

But one thing she had to be sure of. For Luca. And if Rodriguez couldn't handle it, she would walk away, no matter how disappointed her father was. No matter how much compound interest in guilt it earned her.

"Will you adopt him?"

Rodriguez stiffened, his posture totally rigid. "What?"

"Will you adopt Luca? Give him your name. The same name I will have. The same name his half-brother or -sister will have. Will you make him a part of this family? Because if not, I'll walk away now."

A muscle in Rodriguez's jaw twitched. "I cannot name him as my heir."

"I don't expect you to. But I cannot have him be alone in that way." Just the thought of it made her throat ache, made it get unbearably tight. "I need him to know that he has a father. That he isn't the only one who isn't a part of a family."

"Having a father can be vastly overrated," Rodriguez said, his voice rough.

"Give him your name. Your protection. And I will marry you. Be your wife in every sense. But you have to make my son yours, as much as your other children."

She watched as his Adam's apple bobbed, his eyes fixed on Luca. "Then I will adopt him after the marriage. All of this can be simple enough. We marry, we produce an heir. We lead separate lives."

"Why?"

He looked past her, at Luca, who was now lying on his back looking at the sky. Then he looked back at her. "Because I'm not after a perfect, happy family. I want to do what is right by my country. What is necessary."

"The way that disrupts your life the least?"

"And yours, Carlotta. You can keep living as you please here. You'll have very little obligation to me. This marriage will be like a job you can clock in and out of. On for public appearances, off when it's done."

"So, I get lovers too, then?"

He shrugged. "What's good for the goose."

"Just not while we're—"

"Mommy!"

She turned sharply and saw Luca, standing right at the edge of the terrace. He had a way of darting from place to place with no warning, her son. It had never really been a problem before.

"Yes, Luca?"

"I'm bored."

"And tired I'll bet," she said.

"No." He shook his head for emphasis, the serious expression on his face reminding her of her brother Alessandro. She was so thankful that he seemed to have none of his father in him.

"Yeah, I don't believe that, *figlio mio*, but nice try," she said, running her fingers through his dark hair, ruffling it.

"There is a room next to yours," Rodriguez said, his manner suddenly awkward. Luca did seem to make him nervous and she wasn't really sure why. "He can stay in there."

"Good. If we could have his things brought in, that would be great."

Rodriguez nodded curtly. "After he's in bed, perhaps you and I can have dinner."

Carlotta wasn't sure how she felt about that. She liked having Luca as a buffer. It was much more comfortable.

Ironic that you feel the need for a buffer since you're planning on having a baby with the man. No buffers then.

That thought had her hot all over. Well, not so much the pregnancy and childbirth aspect of it. She'd hated being pregnant. Every moment of it. It had all been sickness and sadness. A little bit of denial. Only when Luca was placed in her arms had everything truly come together. And from that moment, she'd been lost. Everything that had come before it—the pain, physical and emotional—had paled in comparison to the love that had flooded through her when she'd seen her son for the first time.

She'd already done it once without a man in the picture.

"Great. We can talk more then," she said, wondering if any amount of talking would ever make the situation seem normal.

After spending a couple of hours getting Luca settled and conked out in his new room, Carlotta went back to her room and selected a nice dress from her collection of, admittedly, out-of-date clothing.

Clothes just didn't matter when you hardly ever went anywhere and certainly never went on dates. As Queen of Santa Christobel she would need new clothing....

Oh. *Madre di dio*. She was going to be the Queen of Santa Christobel. She had sort of been stuck on being Rodriguez's wife. On what it would mean to marry him and share his bed, and have his baby, and uproot her son from his home in Italy. She hadn't even gotten to the queen bit.

She tugged the dress off the hanger and sat on the bed in nothing but her bra and panties, the plush, silken comforter billowing around her, enveloping her. She clutched the rust-colored dress to her chest and breathed in deeply, trying to stop the room from spinning.

This was not her life.

And what is? Self-imposed exile in Italy? Living it up, aren't you, Carlotta?

She had known she'd have to get back into the swing of things eventually. Start living life beyond the four walls of her home. She hadn't really intended on doing it in such a grand way.

Life had seemed…still, for the past five years. No, not still. Because Luca always changed. Every day there was something new and exciting for him, and she lived it, loved it. Loved him. But for her…there had been nothing. It had been like being wrapped in a cocoon. Now she was torn from it, and she doubted she'd had any grand transformation.

She didn't know if she was ready for this. And she didn't really have anyone to talk to. Normally she would call Sophia but since she was currently shacked up with Ash in India and Carlotta was now engaged to the man she'd been intended to marry…

Well, she deserved to be dragged into it, all things considered.

Carlotta took her phone out of her purse and tapped the icon on the screen for text messaging. She'd sent Sophia a blistering message when she'd found out she'd run off with Ash. Now, well, she couldn't really blame her younger sister. This was…it was overwhelming. Maybe if Ash had been standing by with a private plane she would have run off with him too. Though she wouldn't have hopped into bed with him.

Hope you're having a blast in India. BTW, I'm marrying the fiancé you ditched. Good choice, he's an ass.

She hit Send on the message, then tapped the screen again, a smile curving her lips. She hit the New Message icon.

He's also a total stud. So that's some consolation.

This time when she hit Send, her smile was smug. She hoped Sophia was happy, whatever she was doing. Well, she had a fair idea of what her sister was doing, since she'd been caught in Ash's bed on his private plane.

Sophia was the one person who didn't seem completely ashamed of her and Luca. But while she wished her sister a lifetime of happiness, and if that included a torrid affair with Ash, fine with her, she deserved a *little* goading, all things considered.

Her phone pinged and she picked it back up. New message from Sophia.

At least our father will be pleased to have both of us marrying fellow royals.

Married? She'd just thought Sophia was sleeping with him. Well, then things really had worked out in her father's favor. One daughter to a maharaja, the other, the one who'd been mired in total disgrace, married off to a prince.

She typed in another quick message. Congrats, Soph. Love ya.

She snorted and tossed the phone onto the bed. Yes, this was all working out great for Eduardo Santina. Hopefully it would work out even half as well for her.

There was a sharp knock on her door and she scrambled from the bed, stepping into the dress and contorting her arm so that she could tug the zipper up. "Just a second."

She got it midway up, then reached over her shoulder and grabbed it from above, tugging it up the rest of the way. She looked in the mirror and pulled on the neckline, trying to make sure everything was in its proper place. Her figure was a bit fuller since her pregnancy and sometimes she wasn't quite sure what to make of her new curves.

Not that they were pin-up worthy or anything. But at least she could fill out the top of her dress now, with a little cleavage.

She wondered what Rodriguez would think. If he would check her out. That made her cheeks feel hot. She tried to find some hold on her control, tried to keep in command of her body's reaction.

This is what happens when you give in. When you're weak.

That was what her father had shouted at her the day she'd told him she was pregnant. The day she'd told him who the father of her baby was through heartbroken sobs. It was so easy to feel the shame, the sick, crawling feeling of dirt on her skin, as she confessed the truth about Gabriel.

She was determined never to be weak again.

"Ready," she said, turning away from her reflection, redirecting her thoughts.

The door swung open and Rodriguez was there, leaning against the frame. *He* didn't look last season, not even close.

His crisp, white shirt was unbuttoned at the collar, revealing a wedge of golden brown skin and just a little bit of dark chest hair. His dark hair was disheveled. He looked like a man who'd just come from his lover's bed.

She wrinkled her nose. She'd been upstairs for a couple of hours, it was entirely possible that he'd…

"So, how was your evening?" she asked, stepping past him, out into the corridor.

"Fine. I had some work to see to."

"Great."

"You?"

"Luca seems settled in. I don't know if he really understands that we're staying here. But then, I guess that makes two of us."

"Three," he said, walking ahead of her, taking the stairs two at a time. She followed as quickly as her kitten heels would allow.

"You don't feel at home here?"

He stopped at the bottom of the stairs and looked up at the painted ceiling. "I never have."

"You could…redecorate."

A short laugh escaped his lips and he stuffed his hands into the pockets of his dark slacks. "That's almost like suggesting I paint over the Sistine Chapel's ceiling. I mean, not quite, but as far as Santa Christobel and our history is concerned, it is."

"Well, that would be a bad idea then."

"Very likely."

He paused and turned to her, placing his hand on her lower back. She felt the heat of his touch blaze through her, like fire had ignited in her bloodstream, moving through her like a reckless spark on dry tinder.

Was she so desperate for a man's touch that such a simple thing could turn her on so quickly? Well, clearly she was. A man she didn't even know, a man she wasn't sure she liked. She truly was no better now than she'd been six years ago. It was still there, that reckless passion. The one she'd worked so hard to shove down deep, to lock away forever. It was a sobering, gutting realization.

"This way," he said, unaware of the turmoil his hand on her back had caused.

She kept her shoulders straight, tried to keep it

so his hand only touched the fabric of her dress and didn't press it down so that it came into contact with her back again. Because that had been far too disturbing.

The dining room was as opulent and formal as the rest of the house, the sprawling ceiling mural continuing through, with scenes of a massive feast painted just above the long, expansive table.

"Cozy," she said.

That earned a laugh from Rodriguez. "Isn't it? Perfect for an intimate dinner for two. Plus twenty."

"The palace in Santina is a bit like that. It's daunting. Luca…he's not used to this."

"Why did you take him away from Santina?"

"The press," she said, her voice soft.

He pulled a chair out for her and she sat, touching the golden fork that was set beside an ornate dinner plate.

"It was bad for you?" Rodriguez took his seat opposite her.

She looked nice tonight, pretty even. She dressed too plainly for his taste, her hair too well ordered and smooth for his liking. But she was attractive, more than he'd given her credit for the first time he'd seen her.

She looked up, her green eyes hard. "I have the only illegitimate child in the entire Santina family. Going back generations."

An incredulous laugh escaped him. "That anyone has ever owned up to. Do you honestly think there haven't been others?"

"My father said…"

"I'm sure there are descendants of Santina bastards all over Europe. It's the nature of things."

She gritted her teeth, her eyes suddenly bright with rage. "My son is not a bastard."

"That isn't what I meant."

"Pick your words a bit more carefully then."

She had teeth. And claws. Neither of which he'd seen in the interaction with her father. However, when it came to the boy, she was fierce. Good. It would make her a good mother for his heir. Protective. Strong. Something that had certainly been lacking in his life.

She would be a good queen too. While he found her a bit plain, it would suit her position. She had that regal quality to her. He preferred a sex-on-legs quality when it came to his bed partners, but a wife needed something else entirely. And Carlotta had that something else.

He hadn't fully appreciated it until that moment. "Noted, *princesa*."

"Anyway," she said, looking back down at her empty plate. "That's why I've been in Italy. It's simpler there. I came back for the engagement party. A chance to see someone else mess up."

"You think your brother is making a mistake?"

"In my father's eyes he is. It's petty. But...I don't like being the bad one."

"I've never minded bad girls." He watched her eyes round with shock, and he also saw a spark of interest flash in those green depths. Perhaps his bride-to-be wasn't quite as plain as he had imagined.

Maybe there was more beneath that prim and proper exterior.

It was certainly a fascinating thought. One that caused a flash fire of arousal to roar through his blood. Six months without sex. *Dios*, that was a long time. The longest he'd gone since he was sixteen and he'd found out that life came with some very lush and interesting perks.

Women were just another of the many reasons

he didn't mourn the loss of his childhood. Giving women pleasure, taking his pleasure with them, had provided him with moments of total release. Oblivion. He had always treasured those moments.

"No, you haven't, according to your tabloid reputation," she said. "Which reminds me, and I'm sorry to bring it up just before dinner, do you have a clean bill of health? I mean, have you had a recent physical? Because from what I've read, you've been around."

"Not wrong of you to bring it up," he said, ignoring the unfamiliar prickle of shame. "Being safe is important. And I always am. And it so happens, I have a doctor's report for you."

"I... That's more than I expected."

"It's reality. I've never denied living a certain lifestyle, but I'm careful, and I make sure to protect my lovers. As I will make sure to protect you."

Carlotta felt her body getting hot again. She felt the need to remind herself that she'd done the swept-off-her-feet-and-into-bed-with-a-stranger thing before. And while it had been a glowing, heady few weeks, it had been a cold and stark reality when she'd woken up to the truth about the man she'd given her virginity to. The man who'd left her pregnant and alone.

Well, whether he'd left or not, she would have kicked him to the curb once she learned the truth. He'd just saved her the trouble. And the truth had kept her from tracking him down.

A little sliver of flame wound its way through her body as she studied Rodriguez. She took a deep breath, hoping that might help extinguish it. That she would be able to maintain control over herself.

It was proving to be more difficult than it should.

"And how will you be certain of your health if you're…if you're taking other lovers?" She swallowed. "Don't make a fool of me. If you sleep around, I want to know. Don't ever lie to me."

She supposed in a way, she would deserve a cheating husband. Poetic justice in many ways. She would be the one at home with the children, wondering how her husband's business trip was going while he was really wining, dining and bedding another woman.

She nearly gagged.

"Just don't lie," she said again. That was the

part she couldn't stand. The lies. Being manipulated into believing a man was someone he wasn't. Falling in love with the facade.

He looked at her, his dark eyes unreadable. "You want to know about the other women?"

"I will not be treated like I'm stupid." Even if she was. Even if she had been terminally stupid in the man department at one time. She never would be again.

"I will give you my honesty. What you choose to do with it is up to you, but I will never lie to you. If you want the truth, you can have it."

It would probably be easier to just take her charming husband into her bed when he was home, and ignore him when he wasn't. But she wouldn't live that way. She wouldn't be that woman.

"I do."

"I will have the same, *princesa*."

"Of course. And fidelity while we are trying to conceive is non-negotiable. You are not having me and a harem at the same time."

"You are not quite what I expected." He leaned back in his chair and appraised her, his gaze open, honest as he said he'd be. He didn't bother disguising the fact that he was assessing her. Didn't bother to hide it when his eyes dropped to her breasts.

And she couldn't suppress the mild bit of satisfaction she took in him checking her out.

"Well, of course I'm not," she said, trying to ignore the little of prickle of heat that was starting at her scalp and migrating down. "You were expecting to marry my sister. We're not even remotely similar. She's shorter for one thing."

"And quieter, if I remember right. Though I don't know that I ever engaged her in conversation."

"You're hardly marrying for the conversation though, are you?"

"You're more engaging than I imagined you to be, it might actually have just moved up on my list of desirable qualities in a wife."

"Good thing, because you appear to be stuck with me."

"And you like making…conversation?"

"I'm a little bit out of practice making any kind of conversation that doesn't involve the physical ailments of stuffed animals, or require me to refer to myself as Mama."

She noticed a little bit of tension in his brow, the lines of his handsome face tightening. For all his carefree manner, there was more to Rodriguez than he showed the world. Although she wasn't sure if it was better than what he did show.

"So," she said, clearing her throat and tapping the dinner plate with her fork. "Are we…eating?"

As if on cue a man came in carrying a tray with two plates on it, which he set on top of the fine china in front of Rodriguez and in front of her.

"Paella del mar," he said. "I hope you like shell-fish."

"It would be sacrilege if I didn't. Santina is a part of the sea. It's the life force of the country."

"As it is here in Santa Christobel. That, at least, should be similar to your home."

She looked down at the rice and pushed the shell of a muscle with the tip of her fork. "Santina hasn't been my home for a long time. How will your people feel about this?"

"About what?"

"You marrying a woman who has a child. Clearly, I'm not your standard-issue virgin princess."

"I doubt my people are under the illusion I have

any desire for a virgin princess. I'm certainly not a virgin, neither do I pretend to be one."

For some reason, his immediate dismissal of the idea gave her a strange rush of pleasure. She shouldn't care whether he approved of her or not, and yet, for some reason, it satisfied her to know that he hadn't really expected, or cared, if his bride were pure as the driven snow.

"What you desire, and what's expected, are two very different things."

"I assume you're an expert?"

"I can claim a bit of experience in the area, yes," she said. She really didn't want the conversation to go in that direction. Someday, maybe. But not now. She was fairly certain her brothers didn't even know the circumstances surrounding Luca's birth. She wasn't really eager to spread it around. "I'm just not certain what your people will make of you taking a single mother as your bride."

"I didn't ask them," he said simply, taking a bite of paella.

"That simple?"

"I am to be their king."

"But there are appearances to worry about and…appearances." Appearance was of the upmost importance to her father. Her mother and father conducted themselves with an old-world grace. They maintained an aristocratic distance from their people, and from the press, that was rare in the modern era. At least, they had. Until she had shattered some of that respectability with a very high-profile, undeniable mistake.

She knew her father might have forgiven her for her mistakes, but he'd never forgotten them. *She'd* never forgiven herself for it. And here Rodriguez was talking as though appearances didn't matter?

"Do you honestly think I care about the way the media sees me? The way the people see me? I have done well for them, and while my father has been fading from this world I have already been seeing to the duties of the king. I will continue to do well for them, to make the country prosper. I will marry and I will continue the line. No more can be asked of me."

"Just because you…said so?"

"Yes, just because I said so."

"And you'll adopt Luca."

"I will give him my name, as I said I would. I keep my word, *princesa*."

"I don't have a great track record with men and

their word," she said, regretting the words as soon as she spoke them.

"On this you can trust me, Carlotta," he said, his voice low, sincere, the mocking edge to his lips gone. "I don't play with people. Power is one of those things that can make a man feel invincible. It can make him feel as though he's entitled to harm those he sees as beneath him. I am everything that the press says I am. The stories are all true. So yes, I have some sins to my credit. But I don't hurt people. I don't lie."

Carlotta looked at him, at his dark eyes, and she felt her heart rate speed up. "I believe you."

CHAPTER THREE

"MY JEWELER will be arriving later."

Carlotta looked up from the drawing Luca had just handed her and nearly choked as she watched Rodriguez walk into the playroom. The staff had spent the afternoon furnishing and arranging everything. Now Luca was fully equipped with a new bed for his room, a small table and chairs, where he was currently sitting, coloring, and a matching, hand-carved toy box for his most prized possessions. Although his favorite stuffed owls held pride of place on a shelf by his bed.

"What jeweler? What for?" she asked, the answer landing about the time the words left her mouth.

"For your ring."

She looked back down at the paper. "Right."

Luca turned in his chair. "Hi."

Rodriguez attempted a smile, his jaw tightening. "Hi, Luca."

"Why do I need to see the jeweler?"

He lifted one dark brow, his focus shifting back to her. "So you can choose the ring."

"Well, I don't see why I really need to choose it."

"Do you have a crown?" Luca asked, his green eyes still fixed on Rodriguez.

Rodriguez looked back at Luca, a flash of discomfort crossing his handsome face. "There is a crown. One that has been in the Anguiano family for a long time. But I don't wear it."

"I would," Luca said, turning back to his drawing.

Rodriguez's brows locked together. "What were you saying?" he asked, his dark eyes not leaving Luca.

"I don't see why I need to choose the ring." Carlotta bent and set the picture down on the table, then straightened. "I mean, it's a ring."

"Your engagement and wedding ring."

"Yes, but it isn't as though…" She looked down at Luca and frowned. "Luca, I'm going to go talk to Rodriguez for a moment."

Luca looked up. "But I'm going to color."

"That's fine, just stay at the table. Color on the

paper only. Out here." She stepped out into the corridor and Rodriguez followed, pulling the door mostly closed behind him.

"You don't seem to be distracted by Luca's interjections," he said.

"He's a kid. He does that."

"I would not have been permitted to do that."

She crossed her arms beneath her breasts. "And you don't think he should be allowed to?"

"There is very little from my childhood I would use as a model when raising a son. I don't mind his comments. I'm just not used to it."

"Oh." She relaxed her stance. "I was saying it's not like our marriage has a whole lot of significance. You intend to do as you please. It isn't as though the ring will have any real value to me."

"You'll want it to match your style, *si*?" he asked.

"I suppose but…"

He frowned, his forehead creasing. "Why aren't you pleased?"

"Pleased?"

"You get to look at diamonds and pick your favorite. Women like that."

She shrugged. "I've had a lot of diamonds."

Jewelry didn't mean anything. It was money, money could buy a lot of things. Jewels sent to her at birthdays and holidays while her family stayed hundreds of miles away, that didn't do a lot to offer comfort.

"And you do not want…more?"

"Does it bother you?" she asked.

"I thought this would please you," he said, his tone exasperated.

"I didn't say I was displeased, Rodriguez. I just…I didn't know you were going to the trouble of having a jeweler come with a display for me to peruse. I wasn't expecting it. Neither do I require it."

"Let me give you something," he said. The tone in his voice changed, there was something different there, something dark. She didn't truly understand it, but in some ways, she doubted if he did either.

"I'll choose a ring. But you are already giving me something. You're giving Luca your name. It…it means a lot to me. The Santina name has been nothing more than a curse to him in so many ways. Because him bearing my last name marks him. No matter how much I wish it didn't," she whispered the last words, the pain strangling her. Whenever she thought of what she'd done to her son, to his life, with her bad decisions, it made her feel like she was bathing in the shame of it all over again. In the agony.

He deserved a mother who made better choices. Her mother and father deserved a daughter who made better choices. At least in this marriage to Rodriguez, she had a small shot at redemption.

Not just for herself. For Luca. For him, bearing the Anguiano name would erase so much stigma from his life. In time, people might forget. He might stop being punished for *her* sins.

That alone made the marriage worth it.

"I don't know if my family name will serve him any better," Rodriguez said.

"It will."

Their eyes met and Carlotta felt the impact like a punch to her stomach, making her breath shallow, her entire body tense. There was something about him, something beyond the masculine beauty of his face, the perfectly square jaw, the dark, compelling eyes. He possessed a kind of sexual magnetism. The sort of charm that could make a woman lose her mind, and her clothes, in less time than it would take for him to properly execute a pickup line.

She could feel her body changing. Her breasts getting heavy, her limbs trembling, her stomach tightening, an ache building in her core. All it took was a look. He didn't have to speak, didn't have to move, and her body was ready for him. For his touch.

How did he do it? How did he peel her control away, strip by strip, like a flimsy silk covering? Not even Gabriel had been able to do that. She'd made the decision to cast off propriety and have an affair with him. With Rodriguez…she was trying to ignore it. Trying to hang on, and yet she couldn't.

She backed away, gripping the knob on the playroom door, counting on the reminder that her son was right there to be her lifeline, to be her link to sanity.

"I'd better go check on Luca."

He nodded sharply, his eyes never leaving hers. "I'll send one of my staff up to sit with him in a couple of hours when the jeweler arrives. Is that all right with you?"

She nodded, not trusting her voice. It might

come out all breathy and shivery. She certainly felt shivery. She backed into the playroom and closed the door behind her, trying to ignore the steady pounding of her heart.

She knew about men like him. Men with charm. Men who made promises with their eyes. Promises of pleasure that young, naive women might mistake for a promise of love.

But the only real promise in men like him was the promise of heartbreak. She knew that. She had the battle scars on her heart, on her life, to serve as reminders.

Rodriguez was a danger, not simply to her heart, but to her control. She had to keep her control. She couldn't afford to let it go. She would give him an heir, and after the wedding, she would give him her body. But it would only be for that purpose.

It could never be anything more.

"Good night, *figlio mio*." Carlotta leaned forward, the cinched waist of her dress digging into her less than toned stomach, and kissed Luca on the forehead.

"Are you going to sleep too?" he asked, his eyes trained on hers. Luca was always so tuned in to her. She imagined it was because it was just the two of them. She poured everything into him. All of her love, all of her energy. It was the most exhausting, rewarding thing she'd ever done with her life.

And now it was changing. Her sweet, peaceful, somewhat boring life. She didn't want it to change. For a moment she just wanted to freeze time. Keep it here, with Luca. With him so small and trusting that his mother had everything under control. His trust in her helped her believe in herself.

But she couldn't stop time. And her control was slipping fast.

"No," she said, trying to force a smile. "I'm meeting with the prince."

"He has a funny name," Luca said.

"Luca! No, he doesn't." Hard for a five-year-old to say though.

"Is he your boyfriend? Elia from school said her mama has a boyfriend."

"Do you even know what a boyfriend is?" she asked, hoping to put off answering the question, since she wasn't really sure what to say about all of this. Rodriguez was...he was nothing to her and her fiancé at the same time, and there was really no clean way to explain that to a child. *She* didn't really understand it.

"No."

"I told you we were going to be living here. And it's because Rodriguez and I are getting married." She sucked in a sharp breath and cursed the tiny zipper of her dress as it dug into her rib cage. "That means he'll be my husband."

"Will he be my dad?"

The thousand-euro question. And she had no clue how to answer it. It also betrayed that Luca did realize it was just them. And that there should be more. That he should have a father. But his father already had a family, and didn't leave any room for them.

Her heart tightened. "Yes, Luca. If I'm married to him, he'll be your dad."

He was adopting Luca, and no matter how involved he was, legally, he would be Luca's father. And she would not let him hurt her son. There was no amount of atonement worth that.

"Good. Where's Sherbet?"

"Here." She reached up to the shelf above his bed and retrieved one of his ratty stuffed owls, much loved and often washed so that his synthetic fuzz was clumped together. "Now, good night, Luca."

"Night," he mumbled, already drifting off to sleep.

She crept from the room and flicked the light off, and nearly ran into the solid figure of Rodriguez when she stepped out into the corridor.

"Madre di dio!" she hissed, her hand on her chest over her raging heart. She would pretend, for now, that her physical reaction was due to him startling her and that it had nothing to do with the fact that he was dressed in a perfectly tailored dark suit that clung to every hard muscle on his lean body. Nothing at all to do with those dark, glittering eyes, the chiseled jaw, the wicked mouth, always curved up as though he was laughing at her expense.

Nope. It was because he'd snuck up on her.

"I have a funny name?" he asked, one dark brow raised.

"You were eavesdropping?"

He shrugged, not even a hint of conscience showing. "Funny kid. He's smart."

She felt a smile tug at the corners of her lips. "He is."

"Lorenzo is here with the rings. Come with me." He looped his arm through hers, a polite gesture. One a visiting dignitary might bestow upon her, back at the palace in Santina. But this was different.

Because every time Rodriguez touched her, it was like throwing a match into a can of petrol. It made her want to escape her own body. To climb out of her skin so she could get away from the heat, and the fire. The desire that made her want to turn to him and put her hands on his chest, to feel if it was just as hard and muscular as it looked.

How did he do this? How did he demolish all of her hard-earned control with just a look?

She hadn't been alone with a man who wasn't a relative since before Luca was born. It was making her hormones a touch unpredictable. And a lot overenthusiastic.

That was why. That was her story and she was sticking to it.

She clenched her jaw tight and followed him down the long, marble-tiled corridor and through double, oak wood doors into a large study. This had a bit of Rodriguez in it. At least, as she imagined him. Large windows that overlooked the turquoise sea and white sand beaches of Santa Christobel. A pale wood desk that had no papers on it, a bright red rug that added punch to the pale color palette.

The desk had a tray on it, lined in black velvet, with at least fifty brilliant rings on display.

"Lorenzo thought we might like some privacy," Rodriguez said, not moving from his position by the doorway. "Go. Look."

Carlotta swallowed and made her way over to the desk. There was a mix of old and new designs, antique mixed with modern. Diamonds in every color, sapphires, rubies.

Carlotta was familiar with fine jewelry. She'd been given her first pair of diamond earrings when she was three. But this...this was different. There was a time when she'd dreamed of a wedding proposal. First from an imaginary suitor, handsome and dashing. And then she'd met the man.

Gabriel. A fitting name. Pale golden hair, beautiful blue eyes. He'd looked like an angel to her.

So perfect. He'd made her heart race and her pulse pound, had made her tremble with the desire for things she'd never really wanted before.

When she'd met Gabriel she'd rushed to throw off the restraints she'd let hold her all of her life. Because he had become the one she'd fantasized about getting a ring from.

Until she'd found out another woman already wore his ring. That thought always brought a kind of sharp, rolling nausea that made her shake, made her body prickle with cold sweat. With disgust. Disgust aimed at herself, for all of the sins her passions had encouraged her to commit.

She closed her eyes, curling her hand into a fist for a moment, fighting old memories. She swallowed hard and forced herself to look back down at the rings. This was different, this, at least, was honest. It wasn't love, but she'd never really had love. She'd been used. She'd been discarded. She'd been tricked.

Even still, she wasn't innocent of every wrong that had taken place in that relationship.

At least now she was going in with her eyes wide-open. At least now her heart wasn't at risk.

"I don't even know where to start," she said. The

gems blurred together as unexpected tears filled her eyes. Why was she being emotional? Because she was thinking about Gabriel? Thinking of him rarely made her cry anymore. It just made her feel sick.

"Start with what you like best." Rodriguez's voice came from right behind her, close enough that she could feel the heat from his body at her back.

She licked her suddenly dry lips and tried to ignore her racing heart. "Help me choose."

"It's not for me, it's for you."

"I know but…" She extended her hand and touched a ring with a white, square-cut diamond at the center. "I don't know."

"Then we'll have to see which one feels right." He reached from behind her, his arm brushing her waist as he picked up the ring she'd just touched. He took her left hand in his and turned her gently, like a dancer might twirl his partner.

She was face-to-face with him, so close now. He held the ring up and handed it to her. She was grateful he wasn't going to put it on for her. She didn't know what she would do if he kept touching her hand. Melt, probably.

Rodriguez watched Carlotta slide the ring onto her finger, her motions smooth and graceful. She was like that. Always. Smooth and dignified. It was hard to imagine her ruffled, even though he'd seen it. Carlotta had a sanguine surface, but when she was cornered, her inner wildcat came out.

He liked it. Even if he couldn't explain why. He tended to like simple women. Not stupid women, but women who had no baggage. Women who just wanted sex and fun. Parties, a night in his bed. And then he always had a gift sent to them later. Something to remember a good time by. It was uncomplicated.

It was enough, because it had to be.

But nothing about marriage was uncomplicated. Even less so when a child was involved. And much less so still when the woman was Carlotta. She had secrets. She had hidden depths. Passion that simmered just beneath the smooth, controlled surface. A passion she seemed to want to deny.

Normally, he wouldn't care about anything hidden. Give him surface. He could enjoy surface forever. But he would be living with Carlotta. Having children with her. Already there was Luca.

It made him want to know.

Her throat convulsed as she looked down at her hand, at the glittering diamond there. "Not this one."

He shook his head. "No, not that one. It's too… expected."

She laughed. "Well, maybe it is perfect. Because generally speaking, I'm expected."

"Why do you say that?" he asked, scanning the tray, his eyes fixing on a gold, ornate band with a pear-cut emerald set in the center.

"I'm here, aren't I? Marrying you, because my father asked me to. Because it was the right thing to do."

"I find that very unexpected," he said, taking the ring between his thumb and forefinger and pulling it from its satin nest.

"Do you?" she asked, green eyes, so close to the color of the gem, locked with his.

"Yes. I don't know very many people who would drop everything in their life to do what was asked of them. Granted, I know several people who would drop everything to marry a prince, but I don't get the feeling my title colored your motives."

"I'm already a princess."

"And you don't live at the palace."

She bit her lip. "No."

"See? Unexpected." He offered her the ring and she took it gingerly, sliding it onto her ring finger.

She held her hand out, her focus on the ring now. "Very unexpected."

When she moved, he caught the scent of her. She smelled like clean skin and soap, a smell he wasn't sure he'd ever noticed on a woman before. Either because it was covered by perfume, or because he'd just never taken the time to notice, he wasn't sure.

He captured her hand, her skin soft and smooth. It was impossible for him not to wonder how it would feel for those delicate, feminine fingers to trail over his bare skin. Impossible not to wonder if her lips would be just as soft. On his lips, his body.

Six months. It had been six months, and his libido was really starting to rebel.

But she wasn't just a woman at a club. Someone to have a night of fun with. She was supposed to be his wife. The Queen of Santa Christobel. Clearing his desk so he could press her back onto the hard surface and have his way with her wasn't the kind of treatment she would be expecting. And anyway, it would scatter the jewelry.

Who cares? You'll be a terrible husband and father, but you could give her this.

Sex. He was good at sex. At making women feel good about themselves. And in the process, it made him feel good.

"I like this one," he said, shutting the images out of his mind.

Her eyes clashed with his. "You do?"

"Do you?"

She nodded. "Yes."

"Then you should have it," he said. "And it only seems fitting that I ask you again. Will you marry me?"

"I…"

He moved his thumb over the back of her hand, relishing the silken quality of her skin. He bent his head and pressed his lips to her knuckles, his eyes never leaving hers. He saw her pupils expand, a strange mix of curiosity and desire mingling in there.

"Say yes," he said, his lips brushing against her skin.

"Yes," she whispered.

He lifted his head, his eyes meeting hers. He saw a sheen of tears there. It made his chest feel tight. Had he made her cry? Was he already a source of unhappiness for her?

"Good." He managed to force the word out.

"Rodriguez…" She took a step toward him, her hand outstretched. And he wanted to draw her to him. To offer her some kind of comfort. To tell her things would be okay.

He took a step back, denying the impulse. This was why he was so intent on them leading separate lives. He couldn't fulfill her needs, not the emotional ones. And why he cared, he didn't know.

He didn't understand this, the tightness in his chest mixed with a strange attraction that had been growing in him from the moment he'd seen her. Slow and steady, not hot and instant. But it was there. Smoldering. Constant. And what he was feeling now, it wasn't easy. It wasn't casual. Maybe that was what happened when you asked a woman to marry you.

"See you in the morning."

He turned and walked from the room, ignoring the hurt he'd seen on her face. He'd done the wrong thing. But it wouldn't be the last time. It was better they both get used to it.

CHAPTER FOUR

"THERE will be a formal announcement of our engagement today." Rodriguez walked into the dining area, where she and Luca were having breakfast, looking respectable in his tailored suit, yet somehow managing to look disreputable at the same time.

Or maybe that was just Carlotta's mind, objectifying him. She'd certainly been doing a fair amount of it lately. She'd been absent any sort of sexual thrills for quite a while, and one thing Rodriguez provided, just by walking into a room, was sexual thrill. So, it wasn't entirely her fault.

Anyway, there were scores of tabloid tales, provided by exes, talking about all his prowess. Prowess she would be experiencing soon.

Her face got hot and prickly.

"How formal? Are you sending an aide or…"

"We're having a press conference."

Carlotta set her coffee cup down on its saucer. "A press-conference press conference? With a room full of reporters and flashbulbs and hideously invasive personal questions? That kind of press conference?"

"If there's any other kind I haven't yet been to it."

Luca took another bite of churro and Carlotta winced as he set it down on the white tablecloth, then planted his sticky, sugar-coated hands on the formerly pristine surface. Rodriguez didn't seem to notice. "What's that mean?"

She waited to see if Rodriguez might answer, but he seemed as oblivious to the question as he'd been to the sugary handprints. Or at least he was pretending to be.

"There will be reporters, people who work for the television news and the paper, and they're going to come and ask Rodriguez and me questions. Take our picture."

"Me too?" Luca asked.

Carlotta shook her head. "No. You would be bored. You'd have to sit still."

Luca frowned. "I'll stay and play with Angelina. She said she had movies." His nanny had arrived late the night before and Luca was thrilled to see her.

Angelina hadn't been full-time when they'd lived in Italy, but she'd agreed to drop her other charges and come to Santa Christobel to live in the palace. Because now life was different. Carlotta had responsibilities outside of her son. It was sort of jarring and depressing.

"Good," she said, her response halfhearted now.

"We only have a couple of hours to prepare," Rodriguez said.

"And why didn't you tell me this last night?" she asked.

"It didn't seem…important." The way he said that, the way his tongue caressed the words, his deep voice almost like a physical embrace, it reminded her of everything that had happened last night. And everything that hadn't. Everything she'd wanted to feel, and then been ashamed for later.

She'd wanted him to do more than kiss her hand. Had wanted to feel the slow glide of his tongue sliding over her skin as he made the contact more intimate. Had wanted to feel the hot press of his mouth on her neck, her lips, down again to her breasts…

It was as though part of her, a part she'd ignored

and forced down deep inside herself, had reawakened. She really, really didn't want that part to wake up. She'd given in to that wild, reckless bit of herself before. The one that had always wondered what it would be like the slide down banisters and run barefoot on the palace lawn when she was a child. The one who wanted to find out what it was like to have a wild, passionate affair as an adult. Oh, yes, she'd given in to that part of herself once. Only once.

And she'd paid for it. Endlessly.

She loved Luca more than her own life, which made it hard to regret everything. But shaming her family like she had, bringing the paparazzi down on her head. The fact that, whether the other woman knew it or not, Carlotta had taken someone's husband into her bed. And her final moments with the man…the ones she could never erase…she regretted all of that bitterly.

It galled still. Made her feel dirty every time she thought of it, as though there was a permanent film covering her skin. One that never washed clean, no matter how many times she showered. No matter how many times she chose the sensible option instead of the risky one. It was always there. Waiting to betray her.

And now that she was experiencing this uncontrollable…thing around Rodriguez, it was coming back stronger than it had been in years. Along with the reminder of what happened when you chose impulse over propriety.

"Well, it is important. I have to get ready."

His lips twitched. "You look fine."

She put her hand to the back of her head to see if the high, spiky ponytail she'd managed early that morning was still there. "No. I don't," she said, after confirming that she was still, in fact, a disaster.

"All right, maybe you should get ready."

She stood, trying to remember all of the grace and poise she'd learned living in the palace in Santina. It was sort of laughable when one had the crazy ponytail and gray sweatpants. Even if they were cute gray sweatpants.

She was going to have to get into the mindset of being on show again. All the time. All day, every day. That was royal life, and even though she'd let herself forget it these past five years, it was still there in her.

Along with a few other things she thought she'd left behind.

She looked down at Luca, who had a ring of sugar around his mouth and half a churro and cup of hot chocolate left to eat. "Can you stay with him while I get myself sorted?" she asked.

Rodriguez looked down at Luca, trying to keep his face blank of emotion. A tough thing to do since his chest was tightening with a strange feeling he was reluctant to identify. Fear. He was afraid of a five-year-old boy. Wasn't that a joke.

"Fine," he said, taking a seat a few chairs away from Luca.

"I'll be back in a bit. I'm good at getting ready fast."

Carlotta walked out of the room, and he felt compelled to watch. The way the loose, gray pants hugged her pert butt when she walked was the biggest tease he'd come across in a while. Because she should have looked plain. Boring. And yet, something about her face scrubbed free of makeup, and her hair so obviously unstyled was…eye-catching. He had to look twice. A third time.

And he'd had to watch her walk—sashay, really—from the room like she was in her finest dress and heels, when she was wearing slippers and sweats. Shockingly, he'd found a lot to look at.

"I like these."

Rodriguez turned his head, Luca's little voice as effective as a bucket of cold water in his lap. The arousal that had tightened his gut eased and the tightness in his throat returned.

"Do you?" he asked, assuming Luca meant the churro he was holding up in his little hand.

He nodded. "I like this table too. It's big. I bet you could fit a really big cake on it."

Rodriguez looked at Luca, not sure of what he was supposed to say to that. The boy just kind of…chattered. About cakes and crowns and whatever came to his mind. It didn't make him angry. That kind of thing would have made his father angry. As a result, he hadn't chattered much, and he'd never been around children who did.

He'd never really been around children at all, not even when he was one.

Dios. He was actually sweating. Small beads of cold moisture forming on his brow, his back. Being near Luca made it so easy to remember…

"I like chocolate cake. With sprinkles. It's what I had for my last birthday. And I got Sherbie and Sherbet."

Rodriguez sucked in a breath. "And they are?"

"My owls. They aren't real. They're toys."

"And he thinks *I* have a funny name," he muttered.

"What?"

"Are you going to school this year?" he asked. That seemed safe. And normal. Not something random about stuffed animals.

"I don't know. I was going to, but Mama said that now I might not. I might have school here. Because it's different to live in a castle."

Images of his own childhood, lonely, with no one but adults around him. On a good day, a stern nanny or teacher. And then there were days when there was only his father.

"It can be," he said slowly, his eyes meeting Luca's. "But it can be fun." He wasn't sure if that was true. All of his fun had been away from the castle. Well, that wasn't entirely true. He'd discovered women here, at a much too early age. They had been a revelation. A way to feel happy.

He frowned. He knew already he didn't want

that for Luca. Growing up fast had been a must for him, but the thought of this boy behaving like he had in just ten short years…that didn't settle well with him.

He tried again. "If you want to go to school away from the palace, we can arrange it." Luca nodded and Rodriguez wasn't at all sure he'd understood what he was saying. "I mean, you can stay here for school if you want." He looked over his shoulder and at the door Carlotta had walked out of only a few short moments ago. "Or you could go to a class with friends."

"I think it would be more fun with friends."

"I'm sure it would be." Rodriguez couldn't comment on that for sure either. "We'll talk to Car— your mama."

Luca's nanny, a petite redhead with pale skin and freckles, walked in, a smile on her face. "Good morning, Your Highness," she said, her focus on him, her smile bright. "And good morning to you too, Luca."

Rodriguez stood, hoping the swiftness of the motion didn't betray just how eager he was to get out of the room. "*Buenos dias*. You must be Angelina."

"I am," she said, clasping her hands behind her back. She was cute. In a flashier way than Carlotta, thanks to her fiery red hair and glittering golden eyes. Not so long ago, a week ago, he would have been tempted to make a pass at her.

But now he thought she didn't quite measure up to Carlotta's quiet sophistication. Carlotta was…sleek. Her hair always so neat, except for this morning, her appearance always perfectly pressed. Again, except for this morning. And that added dimension had only made her more interesting. She had layers. He couldn't remember ever caring if a woman had layers before.

Strange.

"Nice to meet you. I have…"

"The press conference," she said, moving to the table and sitting right next to Luca. He should have done that. Not sat with three chairs between them as though the boy were a leper.

"Yes. The press conference." He took one last look at Luca, who had his serious green eyes trained on him. "I'll…I'll see you later, Luca."

Luca brightened, a smile curving his small mouth. "Bye."

Rodriguez turned and walked out of the room, trying to ignore the uncomfortably tight feeling in his chest.

For Carlotta, the press held about as much appeal as a food-borne illness and all the charming symptoms that came with it. They were, in her estimation, beneath contempt. People who preyed on the mistakes and tragedies of others, weaving them into salacious stories for the consumption of a scandal-hungry public.

Walking into a room full of the vultures was about the lowest thing on her to-do list. Still, she was doing it. In style too. With the kind of heels normally reserved for…well, never. She'd gotten out of the habit of wearing high shoes when pregnant with Luca. Then after he was born, carrying him in heels was about as practical as waddling around in heels with a big pregnant belly.

So, her fabulous, sky-high black stilettos had been on hold in the back of her closet for years, and now, paired with a sedate, but cheery, yellow sheath dress, she was looking quite…well, almost sexy, in an understated way. It was a welcome break from her typically sedate appearance. At least, that's what she was telling herself.

She took a deep breath and started down the long corridor that led to the room they were holding the conference in. She was confident. Strong. Sexy—at least, she had been in another life, and was trying it out again. She could do this.

She lengthened her strides and tipped her chin up, the razor-blunt edges of her hair skimming her shoulders. Yes, she could do this. She was strong, sexy and in control.

She rounded the corner and ran into Rodriguez's broad frame, her breasts and tipped-up chin hitting the hard wall of his chest and his neck, respectively.

"Oh, I'm sorry! This is… I'm sorry," she said, fighting the urge to ramble. When had she become so…not a princess? Just clumsy and coming to breakfast in her sweats and…and she couldn't do that now. She was in a palace. She was marrying Rodriguez.

She had to change. Again. Just when things had been getting really comfortable it was all changing again.

Oh, no. Not this, not now. Tears were stinging

her eyes, her throat tight and aching. This was not the time for an emotional breakdown.

He put his hands on her shoulders, his dark brown eyes meeting hers, sending a little zing of electricity through her. "It's fine."

She swallowed hard. "I don't…I don't really want to do this."

His brows locked together. "Are you okay?"

"It's just…" She blew out a breath and waved her hand. "Me. And the media. I don't like to be in the news."

He frowned. "Because of Luca?"

"Because of what they did to me when they found out I was pregnant with Luca. Do you have any idea…?" She blinked and looked away. "It was horrible. They followed me everywhere. Crowding me while I ate. I was sick all the time anyway and to have a camera shoved in my face while I was just trying to have a relaxing meal… and there were pictures of me walking with my belly circled, drawing attention to it, along with the flattering headline *Who's the Father?* And when they realized we weren't telling them, they switched to things like *Has Princess Carlotta Put on Too Much Baby Weight?*"

His thumbs moved up and down, from her satin-covered shoulders down to the bare skin of her arms. "I know. It's a necessary evil though. The way I can communicate with my people. They've written…I don't even know what all they've written about me. Things about my exploits. Most probably true, but not something I want to read in black and white. Not something I'd want my maiden aunt to read."

"Do you have a maiden aunt?"

"That was for illustrative purposes. The point is, the press is a part of royal life, of our lives. I employ a 'keeping my enemies closer' strategy with the media."

"And does it work?"

He smiled, that wicked half-smile of his. "I have no idea, I don't read that sort of thing, remember?"

"You mentioned."

He slid one hand down her arm, warm fingertips trailing over her skin before he took her hand in his. "Now, let's go have a press conference."

Her heart started moving to its own rhythm, too fast, too hard, to be normal. Why did he have to be charming? Or, the bigger question, why did it work on her? Why did it make her stomach tighten, her nerve endings sizzle, when she knew how easy this kind of charm came to men like him?

She didn't know why. She only knew it did.

"Okay, I'm ready."

His smile widened, and as it did, she felt something in her chest expand. "Good. Now, try not to run into me on your way in."

CHAPTER FIVE

"WHERE did he propose?"

This question came from one of the reporters in the front, directed at Carlotta, who seemed stiffer than usual at his side. He'd gotten a glimpse of the depth of her discomfort in the hallway. Visible cracks in that smooth veneer of hers.

"He… In his office," she said.

It was true, even if it was a very unromantic picture to paint for the press. Not that he really cared. The press would take what they said and do whatever they pleased with it. That was how it worked. They didn't get a vote on how they were portrayed in the media. He'd given up caring years ago.

But Carlotta cared. He could see it, in her stance, in the tenseness in her body. She cared a lot.

"You make it sound dull, Carlotta, when we both know it wasn't." He turned to her and brushed his thumb over her cheek gently, fascinated by the stain of pink that spread over her cheeks, beneath her smooth golden skin.

"Of course it wasn't," she said, her voice stronger now. "But I didn't want to give away the entire story. You were so sweet and romantic."

Her comment made his breath rush out on an involuntary chuckle. "All right. Then we won't tell them about the doves." He tossed the crowd of reporters a look. "Boring story. Next question?" With any luck, their little display would have the reporters writing about secret glances and shared jokes.

"Prince Rodriguez, you're the first ruler in the Anguiano family to marry a woman who already has a child. What does that mean for the country? Are you concerned about watering down the line?"

He heard Carlotta suck in a sharp breath and a strong surge of some unidentifiable emotion rose in his chest. It burned. He felt like there was a pool of fire in his chest, and if he gave it free rein it would take over. And if it did…he did not know what he would do.

Teeth clenched, he forced words forward. "Luca is a child, not an incidental. He is off-limits. Next question, and if you cannot keep it on a topic I approve of, we can be finished here."

More questions followed, about the wedding date, how they met. All of which he glossed over with practiced ease.

"I think that's enough for one morning," he said.

"Pictures?" A photographer stood up in back.

Rodriguez nodded his head once in affirmation and drew Carlotta to his side, his arm wrapped around her waist. She felt cold. The fire in his chest kindled again. He leaned in, his lips touching her ear. "Try to smile."

She turned to him, her mouth only a whisper from his, her full lips looking soft and more tempting than he could remember lips ever looking. He wanted to kiss her. And his mind was going no further than that. The need for a simple kiss…he couldn't remember ever wanting that.

But this wasn't the time.

He turned to the photographers and offered a smile. Carlotta did the same, her head angled just perfectly toward him, almost as though she were deferring to him. They made quite a picture. A royal couple who looked better than his parents ever had, for the short amount of time they'd been a couple.

At least in pictures they looked like all Santa Christobel would expect of a ruler and his queen. Maybe these images would blot out the ones they'd looked at for years. Pictures of him with leggy blondes in tight skirts, driving fast cars, leaving notorious nightclubs. And then, one of their favorite sequences, he and a date entering a luxury hotel in the early-morning hours, him leaving a couple of hours later, and his date, dashing out in the daylight hours, wearing the same thing she'd worn the night before.

They loved that one. A look at the scandalous prince. After a while, reading his own exploits had bored him. And sometimes it made him...

He shut his mind on the thoughts. This wasn't the time to reflect on all of that. Standing in the formal reception hall, the state seal behind him, his fiancée at his side, it made it seem like another life.

"Thank you," he said, nodding again and dropping his arm from Carlotta's waist. He moved to exit and she stayed with him, walking closely beside him.

She really was the perfect royal wife. At least in public. That was all that mattered.

As soon as they were outside the room, Carlotta seemed to deflate as she released the breath she'd been holding. "That was…"

"I know. I'm sorry that man mentioned Luca. It was out of line. I won't tolerate it."

"Thank you," she said, her voice muted. "Thank you for standing up for him. I know that you aren't… I know you don't really like kids."

"What? Who said I didn't like kids?"

"He makes you uncomfortable. I can tell."

Rodriguez shifted, a vague feeling of…embarrassment, something he wasn't sure he could ever remember experiencing, washing through him. "That doesn't mean I don't like children. I have no experience with them."

"You've never dated a woman who had a child?"

Vaguely, he remembered that there had been a woman who'd left the hotel before him once. He was almost certain she said something about needing to get back so her babysitter could go home. "I… Not one that ever introduced me to her children."

Carlotta began to walk down the corridor, back

to the private palace quarters. He followed, his eyes drifting to the rounded curve of her backside. His body most definitely approved of the view.

"I didn't have any experience with children either. I don't remember if I'd ever held a baby until I held my own. And then, he was so tiny and perfect…I loved him right then. And I knew I didn't need any experience. I just needed to love him." She tossed him a glance over her shoulder. "Of course, I now go through intermittent, crippling bouts of wondering whether or not I'm doing the right thing for him, but, essentially, I trust that just…loving him is enough."

He stopped walking for a moment. "Do you think all mothers feel that when they hold their babies?"

She stopped too, turning to face him. "I…I don't know. It was so strong for me. I know my own mother…she loves us, but she's…she's distant."

"Not as distant as mine, I bet," he said. "I haven't seen her since I was younger than Luca."

"That's… I'm sorry."

He shrugged. "I'm not. I don't do regret."

Carlotta looked at Rodriguez's face. The teasing smile was gone from his lips, but there was no regret in his expression. No longing or sadness. Just blank acceptance. The absence of emotion there was nearly frightening, like she was seeing past the veil, just for a moment, and into the man. That beyond his humor and easy manner there was a deep, dark void, one barely covered by a thin veneer that was in danger of being stripped away at any moment.

It was an insight she wanted to turn away from. An insight she longed to ignore, pretend she'd never seen. But she wasn't sure she could.

"Well, I am," she said. "Even though my mother and father can be difficult sometimes, I do love them."

"Your father basically sold you into marriage, and you call that love?" he asked, a hard note lacing his voice, stripping the velvet off his normally enticing tone.

"Because he needed me. I'm royalty, a different set of responsibilities comes with that. You ought to know all about it."

"And you're doing your penance, right?" He seemed determined to make her angry, and it was working. It was working really, really well. It was easy to forget he'd just stood up for Luca. Easy now to just let all of the goodwill she'd allowed to build up between them slip right through her fingers, while clinging tightly to everything she'd tried so hard to ignore.

The helplessness, the sick, awful feeling that came with being used. The sense that she was little more to anyone than a pawn to be moved around on a chessboard.

And the anger. That was the easiest to latch on to.

"I'm doing the right thing," she hissed. "Maybe I haven't always. But I'm doing it now. Even though it means a lifetime of this." She waved her arm, indicating the palace itself. Including Rodriguez in the sweep. "Because there's more to life than just being happy, or satisfying base urges, or following your passions, whatever they might be at any given time. It's about responsibility."

"Perhaps. Why do you think I'm here? Why do you think I'm even in Santa Christobel and not in my apartment in Barcelona with a redhead? Responsibility. Don't assume I don't understand. But my sense of duty is not driven by guilt."

"Well, it's easy for you, isn't it? Don't you plan

on just going along like Luca and I never happened to you?"

He paused for a moment, a muscle in his jaw jumping. "I did. But you seem pretty determined to make that an impossibility." He advanced on her, his eyes locked with hers. She held her ground, mostly because she didn't want to escape him. Whatever he had in mind, it didn't scare her. It made her body feel tight, even while her muscles seemed to melt into pudding.

"What exactly does that mean? And do you expect an apology?" she asked, crossing her arms beneath her breasts, hoping that bracing herself like that might keep her body from trembling.

"No, princess, not an apology." He stopped, just inches away from her, then he leaned forward, his palm flat on the wall behind her. She expected him to kiss her, to grab her, for his mouth to crash down on hers.

Her heart was trying to climb up her throat and escape, her pulse pounding so hard she felt dizzy, expectation and a huge helping of longing overtaking her senses. But there was no taking. No crashing.

He extended his hand, drew his finger along

the line of her jaw, from her chin to just beneath her ear, the move slow and sensual, intoxicating. Then he brought his other fingers into play, sliding down her neck, his touch featherlight as it skimmed her sensitive skin. His hand drifted down, playing over the line of her collarbone, stopping right at the swell of her breast.

Her eyes clashed with his, the dark intensity she saw there drawing the knot of arousal that was building in her to even more extreme levels. Her body felt heavy, a sharp pain building and spreading at the apex of her thighs. What she wanted, and how quickly she had gotten to the point of wanting it, shocked her.

She'd never been a hot and fast girl. She needed time. But those few brushes of his fingers had been equivalent to thirty minutes of good foreplay. She had to make the decision that it was what she wanted. There was no way for her to make a decision now. She was helpless. Completely swept up in the desire she felt for him.

She just wanted him to close the distance between them. To push her roughly against the wall and let her feel the hardness of his body against hers…in hers.

Ultimately, she was the one that moved, the one who angled her head so that her lips could touch his. Heat exploded in her as soon as their mouths met, a hot, reckless urgency overtaking her.

His kiss was hungry, but hers was starving. She needed it like air, with a desperation she hadn't known lived in her. She planted her hands firmly on the back of his neck, fingers lacing through his thick dark hair as she held him captive against her.

He kept one hand flat on the wall, the other on her lower back, his large hand splayed over her, his heat so perfect and wonderful and not enough.

When they parted, it was with a moan of disappointment from her. His breath was coming in short, sharp bursts, and she was really glad to see it. To know he'd been affected too.

"That," he said, his voice rough, "that is what makes you hard to ignore."

Her stomach tightened, this time not with pleasure. She hated this. That he was able to demolish all of her barriers like this. That he brought up the hot, fiery passion in her that she'd fought for so long to ignore.

Hadn't she learned anything? Rodriguez was going to marry her, but he would be just as faithful of a husband as Gabriel had been to his wife. The only difference was that instead of being the bit on the side, she'd be the one raising his children, keeping the household and family going while he was off pleasing himself.

Was that why Gabriel's wife had stayed? Because Gabriel had her, body and soul, while she had nothing of him but his passing, occasional sexual interest?

And was that what Rodriguez would do to her?

No. It wouldn't happen. She wouldn't let it.

But she feared that with Rodriguez, the choice might not be hers. Because he didn't simply test her willpower. He smashed it into a million pieces. Pieces that were so tiny she feared she might never be able to assemble it again.

"I'll bet you say that to all the girls," she said tightly, turning from him and walking down the corridor. Away from him. Away from the temptation he represented.

And she tried to fight the depression that was creeping over her like fog, drowning out the lingering arousal and leaving in its place the stark realization that time and experience hadn't changed her. She hadn't truly mastered that wild, passionate part of herself. She'd simply managed to hide it for a while. She wasn't in control, and Rodriguez seemed to be out to prove it.

Madre di dio. Things could not get any worse.

"Are you serious? A birthday party?" Carlotta looked at Rodriguez and tried to ignore the slight fluttering that seemed to be taking place everywhere in her body.

She'd managed to steer clear of Rodriguez since the press conference, and since the kiss in the hall. She'd seen him, talked to him, but mostly she'd filled the two weeks since by acclimating Luca to his new home, visiting the local school, making a plan for him to attend in September.

But that didn't stop her from wanting him. From staring at him every time they happened to have a meal with him. From fantasizing about him in her bed every night. In the shower the next morning.

She blinked and tried to concentrate on what he was saying.

"It's for one of the heads of state, and it's one of the really fun things we get to do as rulers of Santa Christobel. You know, go stand on hard marble floors eating soggy appetizers until our backs hurt."

Carlotta wanted to melt into the settee she was perched on. She already felt spent. Rodriguez had been at the palace all day and avoiding him was starting to feel like a full-time job. She'd taken Luca to the cinema in the morning and then she and Angelina had taken Luca out to the beach for the afternoon. She currently felt grubby, exhausted and more than a little bit grumpy.

"On such short notice?"

He acted so calm around her. It was irritating. After the stupid fight, the passion explosion, the continued fighting.

She closed that line of thought down. She wasn't going to remember that. It had been two weeks. No. She didn't recall any of it. And her lips did not still tingle. Neither did any other part of her.

"Sorry, I only just got the invitation passed to me, but it really is too important to miss."

It was infuriating, and it shouldn't be, that he seemed entirely unaffected by the kiss-she-did-not-remember. Because he should look tense. Or unsatisfied. Or angry. Just…something. Rather than his typical, easy-breezy self. The mocking curve of his lips had returned.

She blew out a breath. "I know this is what it's like. Public appearance after public appearance. And then, after, you go home and go to your separate bedrooms, then get up the next day and start over. It's what my parents have always done. They're professionals at this."

"So you can do it too. I'm certain of that."

"I'm certain I can…I never wanted to. For a while I thought…" She shook her head. "Sorry, I'm sharing…I don't know what got into me."

He sat in the chair across from her. "I have nowhere to be until 8:00 p.m. Share away."

"Why?" she asked, narrowing her eyes.

"Shouldn't I know? I'm going to be your husband."

"It's boring. But fine. I used to think I would get married for love. That my husband and I would have this grand passion that could not possibly be satisfied by separate bedrooms. I used to want… more than the sterile palace life I was raised in."

"And now you've lost that dream?"

She snorted a laugh. "I lost that dream six years ago."

"Because you got pregnant?"

"Because of the man who got me pregnant. I don't like to call him Luca's father. He's never met him, so how can he be a father? But he…I thought he was the one, you know? I was stupid. I know better now. That's just a bunch of romantic nonsense, it's not reality. This, what we're doing, is so much more meaningful."

"Even though you hate it?"

She sighed. "At least there's a reason. There's something more firm than…love. Whatever that's supposed to be."

"I don't know that I've ever met a woman as cynical on the subject of love as I am."

"Well, now you have. We got distracted in the hall earlier," she said, averting her gaze, "but the real reason I'm doing this isn't about penance. It's about doing something that matters. I can't matter while I'm hiding in exile in Italy. I certainly didn't contribute to the greater good when I started a relationship with *him*. There's more to life than passion. Duty, that's real. Marrying to better my country? Your country? There are benefits to that that no one can take away. It's all so much more permanent than some ephemeral notion of love."

"And lust? What are your feelings on lust?" The teasing light in his eyes was gone again, replaced by something dangerous, that intense darkness she'd sensed in him earlier.

"Lust is unnecessary, certainly nothing to overturn one's life for."

"Lust keeps things interesting," he said.

"And what's the point of lusting after a husband who intends on taking other women to his bed?" she asked, her words clipped.

"That's only sex. Sex is cheap, Carlotta."

She laughed. "Sex has always been very expensive for me. But then, I suppose that's how it is for women."

"I suppose so. Are your brothers virgins?"

"What? I would never, not for any amount of money, ask them, but I can give you a very confident no."

"Your other sisters?"

"I don't…I don't think so…well, Sophia's married now and Natalia…the press wrote about one of her affairs, but it all blew over quickly enough." Carlotta's twin had always been the audacious one. The one who did what she pleased. She laughed off her indiscretions, and the world laughed them off with her. Her parents simply ignored her antics.

And Carlotta had been the good one. The one who'd never done anything without the express permission of her parents. She'd envied Natalia. So much it burned sometimes. She felt like she was on the outside of this glowing sphere her twin lived in. One where she could do whatever she wanted and nothing could touch her, while Carlotta ached to break the chains that held her in place, and couldn't.

Then she'd met Gabriel. And she'd followed her lust, purposefully decided not to care what her parents might think. To embrace the rush for the first time instead of just turning away from it.

And the fallout of that decision made Natalia's behavior pale in comparison. The Sole Santina Bastard. That was her claim to fame.

"So no one in your family is a saint. Why is it you're the bad one? Because you got knocked up?"

His words were stark. But honest. She swallowed. "Wow. Charming."

"Honestly, why are you worse than they are? Is it just that no one has physical evidence of their sexual history? The public has plenty of evidence of mine—they think I'm suave, if a bit feckless, but they like me. No one calls me names or degrades me. And I'd bet none of them do it to your brothers."

"You don't understand…"

"It's hypocrisy. Plain and simple. That's why, in our marriage, if I'm not going to be faithful I certainly don't plan on holding you to our vows."

He was missing the real issue. Sure, some of her being "worse" had to do with her carrying visible consequences of something other people did behind closed doors without anyone else being any the wiser. But the biggest part had to do with the fact that Gabriel had been a married man, with a wife. Children. But admitting that was too…it was too hard. To look Rodriguez in the eye and confess that she'd been seduced by a married man? That she'd been so stupid she'd missed the signs? She'd already had to admit it to her father. He was the only one she'd had to explain anything to. And that was enough.

"So you think women have just as many rights as men when it comes to sex?" she asked.

"I think it's a ridiculous double standard. Men want to have sex with whoever they want while they limit women. Then who are the men going to sleep with?"

"A philosopher," she said dryly.

"Just all for equal rights."

"Wow. Well." She stood from the couch, her insides feeling oddly jittery. "I'm going to go and see if I can find something suitable for tonight."

"It's been taken care of. Come on, I'll show you."

She wished he wouldn't, because she kind of needed a Rodriguez reprieve, but she wasn't about to admit that to him.

"All right, lead on."

She followed him back to her room, her mind going over the conversation they'd had in the study. He didn't look at her any differently for having a child out of wedlock. Her family was so traditional, that she was the only Santina to ever give birth to a bastard had been major news. It had made her mother hardly able to meet her eyes. Had made her father look at her as though she were dirty, something almost beneath contempt at times.

To have someone simply not see that dark mark

on her record...that was something she hadn't thought possible.

It had altered her own parents' perception of her so profoundly she'd assumed everyone must look at her and see a big scarlet *A* branded across her chest, even without knowing the full story.

He pushed open the door to her room and stood there, allowing her to enter first. Rodriguez had that smooth, surface chivalry down to a science. It probably made women melt at his feet. If his dark good looks, hot body and wicked grin hadn't already done the job.

"I went out today and I was driving through downtown when I saw this." He took a garment bag out of her closet. "And it made me think of you."

"Did you go through my things?"

"No, I asked one of the household staff to put it in the closet."

"Oh."

"You don't like it when people go through your belongings?"

"Would you?"

"I don't know. I live alone so I don't have that

problem." His eyes locked with hers. "I did live alone anyway."

"Now you have us."

"And servants. You can never be truly alone in a castle. Even if all of the staff left there would still be ghosts wandering the old dungeon."

"You have a dungeon here?"

He smiled. "You interested?"

A reluctant laugh pulled up from her stomach. "Not really my thing." She took the garment bag from his hand. "You should be used to staff. You lived here when you were a boy."

"Until I was old enough to go to school. When I was eight I went to boarding school."

"That's so young! I could never send Luca away. Not in three years' time. I don't think I ever could."

He looked at her, his eyes blank, that darkness that lay beneath the surface a palpable force. "I liked school."

"Good." She unzipped the back and her mouth dropped when she saw the black lace dress that was nestled inside. "This is…there's not much to it."

"It will look perfect on you."

"I don't flaunt. I'm a mother."

"You are a woman," he said, his voice firm, insistent. "Don't forget that. Whether you're Luca's mother, my wife or the Queen of Santa Christobel, you are a woman and there's no crime in remembering that."

"I...I know that. I remember. How could I forget?" Of course, for her, being a woman was basically a crime. She didn't know what to do with that part of herself. The part that wanted occasions to dress for. The part that wanted a man in her bed. It was easier to simply be Luca's mother and ignore everything else.

"You dress nicely," Rodriguez said. "But not sexy."

She frowned. "I thought my press conference dress was sexy."

"No, *you* were sexy in it. It would only be considered sexy at a tea party."

She looked him over, at his black pants and shirt, so lovingly fitted to his body, making him look dangerous and attractive. "Well, you dress like you're on the prowl."

"I generally am," he said, offering her a crooked smile. "Now go try the dress on."

She shot him a deadly glare and folded the bag over her arm, heading for the dressing room that was just off the main portion of the bedroom. She got out of her beach clothes and tugged the flimsy dress up over her curves.

She contorted her arm and tugged the zipper midway up her back, unable to finesse it all the way up. She swallowed, her throat suddenly dry. So, she'd ask him for help. He was going to see her naked after the wedding anyway. And this wasn't even naked, this was just a partially exposed back. A bathing suit, even a modest one, would show much more than the dress put on display.

But it wasn't so much about the amount of skin as it was about what Rodriguez made her feel.

Well, she wasn't giving him that power. She owned her body, and she wasn't a slave to errant desires.

She opened the door and poked her head out. "Can you zip me?"

The teasing light in his eyes vanished again, like a candle thrust into the wind. He frightened her when he looked like that. Because he lost that easy manner completely and he became someone—

something—else entirely. Dangerous. A predator. And she had the feeling she was the prey.

"Sure," he said, walking to the dressing room door. Her heart pounded in rhythm with his steps and she did her best to ignore it. To ignore the languid heat that seemed to be inside her bones, spreading through her, making her feel weak and shaky.

She turned and braced her hand on the door, anything to disguise the slight trembling in her fingers.

He didn't bother to pretend, even for a moment, that the brush of his skin on hers was accidental, didn't pretend he was simply helping with the last bit of the zipper. His finger trailed up the line of her back, hot and exciting.

She tensed, drawing her shoulders up.

"Relax, *querida*," he said softly, his knuckle brushing against her shoulder.

"Then you're going to have to stop touching me."

She felt his fingers toying with the zip tab, his other hand moving to her waist, his touch light but so…present. She felt it all the way down to her toes and every interesting point in between.

"Not possible if you want me to help you with your dress."

"You're taking liberties," she said, her voice stiff.

"Don't you sound like the maiden in a Regency drama? I quite like it."

"Next you're going to tie me to the railroad tracks…"

"You're mixing your time periods."

She rolled her eyes, then realized he couldn't see her face. "That's beside the point."

"Sorry, but I find it counterintuitive, covering up a woman's skin, I mean."

"You are shameless, Rodriguez."

He put his hands on her arms and turned her, and she sucked in a sharp breath when she stopped, her face inches from his. "I can be," he said.

"Well, I wish you wouldn't. Be…so shameless."

She looked into his eyes, past the glimmer of humor, to the predator. Her body responded. And it wasn't the flight response she should be having. Maybe she wasn't the prey. Maybe she was a predator too. Maybe her body was on the prowl too. Looking for a mate. She looked down, breaking the visual hold he had on her.

"If you really wish, Carlotta." He moved his hands, reaching behind her and tugging her zipper into place. "I think the dress looks perfect." He took a step back, as though they hadn't just been caught in the most sexually tense moment in the history of sexual tension.

She swallowed hard and turned to face into the dressing room so that she could see herself in the full-length mirror. The dress wasn't really as indecent as she'd imagined—the black lace gave hints of skin, but, thanks to the lining beneath, covered anything that really mattered. It was long, a mermaid-style skirt that flared out past her knees, swishing as she walked.

"It's beautiful," she said, hating to admit he was right. Not enough to give up the dress, but enough.

"I knew it would be."

"A man with much confidence," she said.

"No. How could it be anything but stunning on you?"

She looked at his reflection in the mirror, her eyes meeting his indirectly that way. "Rodriguez, I...I don't need the whole playboy act, okay? I'm marrying you. It's done. You don't need to do this."

She knew, the moment she said the words, that she'd said the wrong thing. His eyes flattened, his mouth thinning into a line.

"If that's what you want," he said, his voice sharp.

"I just… Thank you for the dress."

He nodded and turned, walking out of the dressing room and, judging by the click of the door, her room.

This was why she didn't date. Too messy. And good job, Carlotta, she'd insulted her date right before they were meant to go out. And after he'd given her a beautiful gown.

She wanted to growl in frustration. Instead, she picked up a tube of red lipstick and leaned in closer to the mirror. She was going to chase the sexy look tonight. And maybe, just maybe, she and Rodriguez would manage not to have another fight.

CHAPTER SIX

Sexy didn't begin to describe Carlotta in that black lace gown. It should be illegal. Or they should be alone in one of the expansive bedrooms of the palace, with nothing but free time and an enormous bed at their disposal.

Instead, they were in a crowded ballroom, people everywhere. Normally he enjoyed parties. They were fun, shallow diversions that allowed him to block everything out and focus on nothing but easy, happy things.

Now it was grating his nerves. Because too many people meant he had to behave himself. He wasn't just the rebel prince anymore, he was the future king. He always had been, he knew, but it had all been distant and murky, and he'd been in no hurry to move back into the palace. Back to the source of his darkest moments.

Well, the reprieve was over. Which was how he found himself here, at a party for an octogenarian he'd never met, keeping his hands off of his ultra-desirable fiancée.

"I used to hate these things." Carlotta leaned in, ruby lips brushing his earlobe as she whispered to him. "What's the deal with putting all the food on toothpicks? And honestly, room-temperature shrimp sitting on a tray for five hours?"

He choked a laugh out through his tightened throat. "I can't argue with that."

"I used to hate them," she said. "But now it's been so long since I've been out, I'm finding it really enjoyable."

"What about your brother's engagement party?"

She blinked. "That was…interesting. And stressful. I can kind of see why it made Sophia run off, no offense."

Oh, yes, Sophia. His original intended bride. She never even crossed his mind. It didn't seem right, the thought of another woman standing at his side now.

"None taken," he said, shaking his head when a passing server offered him a shrimp cocktail.

"It was sort of fun watching the Jacksons. They don't care what anyone thinks. It's kind of… refreshing."

"You think?"

She looked at him, green eyes glittering. "I care too much. I've spent so much of my life trying to be who I thought I should be. So yes, it's easy to envy people who clearly haven't got a care in the world about their image."

"Unlike the people here." He surveyed the room, filled with stuffed shirts and black, conservative gowns. "I wonder if any of them have secret lives?"

"Don't we all?" she asked.

"Well, *we* don't. Hard to keep secrets when the press follows you all the time."

"True. Anyway, I like the dress. I'm sorry I fought with you earlier."

"I like the dress too." He'd like it better pooled into a puddle of black lace on his floor, but he would take what he could get.

What was it about her that captivated him? Had he really thought her plain only a few days ago? He hadn't been paying attention, clearly. With her dark hair pulled back into sleek bun, her curves emphasized by the fitted dress, olive skin visible in teasing amounts through the lace and the perfect amount of makeup to highlight her features, she was nothing short of stunning.

"You look beautiful," he said, because that was the kind of thing he said to women. But...he meant it. He always meant it, but usually he was performing a seduction. Words, then touch, then bed. But at the moment, he simply felt it was important for Carlotta to know.

Carlotta didn't want to feel anything when he said that. She knew how men worked. She'd fallen prey to easy lines like that in the past. So she really shouldn't be feeling a rush of heat spreading through her. No flush of pleasure, no rapid heartbeat.

She did though. Because Rodriguez was charming. There was a reason women swooned straight into his bed when he smiled at them. He was hot. And she was celibate.

But she wasn't stupid.

"Thank you," she said tightly.

"You don't like compliments?" he asked.

"I don't like insincere compliments."

"I was sincere."

"I... That's not really what I meant."

A smiling woman whose face looked like it had

been frozen into a permanently surprised expression approached them with her shorter, older husband on her arm. She spoke in rapid Spanish to Rodriguez, and Carlotta could only catch half of it.

"Your new fiancée?" she asked, flashing a smile that showed unnaturally white teeth.

"Sì," Carlotta said, accepting the other woman's double-cheek kiss.

"Muy bonita!" she said.

Rodriguez shot her a look. "I did tell you. Though perhaps you will take Señora Ramirez's word for it?"

Carlotta returned his look with a deadly one of her own before turning her attention back to Señora Ramirez. *"Gracias."*

The *señora* kept talking and Rodriguez translated when Carlotta didn't understand.

"She wants to know when the wedding is," he said, a question in his tone, as if he were wondering the same thing.

"Tell her we're in no hurry." Carlotta looked beyond Rodriguez and felt her heart sink into her stomach.

"I'm in a hurry," he said, his voice hushed, his

hand snaking around her waist, palm resting on her hip.

She cleared her throat. "Well, after my brother Alex gets married maybe…"

That set Señora Ramirez off into a flurry of excited chatter, about invitations and gowns and two royal weddings, how exciting! Her husband just stood next to her, his expression blank.

If Carlotta weren't so overwhelmed, she would probably be fighting back laughter over the poor man's plight. Her own parents were so suitably matched. Both so stoic and regal…well, stoic in public at least. She knew what it looked like when her father was angry. Angry beyond words.

Now she was wishing she'd taken the last passing server up on his offer of room-temperature champagne.…

"Ah, *bailar*." Señor Ramirez spoke for the first time as strains of classical music filled the ballroom.

"I think I am needed now," Señora Ramirez said. "You should dance too." She turned to her husband and the look of pure, undisguised love that passed between them made Carlotta feel like she'd been hit in the chest with a rock.

The way they looked at each other…it told her what she didn't want to believe. That not everyone was cold in their marriage, like her parents. That not everyone lied, like Gabriel. That there was love and happiness.

It would just never belong to her.

You have Luca. That's real love. Permanent love.

"Care to dance, *princesa*?" Rodriguez turned a devastating grin her direction.

No. She really, really didn't. Because it brought back memories of another dance, on another night, and all of her weakness.

"Of course," she said, offering the Ramirezes a smile for good measure.

Rodriguez kept his arm around her waist and they followed the older couple out onto the area in front of the stage that had been kept clear for dancing.

When they were out in the center of it, he pulled her in, clasping her hand in his. "Try not to look so much like you want to chew me out," he said dryly, resting his cheek against hers.

She closed her eyes, sucking in a sharp breath, and just for one moment reveled in the feel of his hard body so close to hers. The light brush of stubble from his face. He was a man. So different from her. His body promised the kind of satisfaction that eluded her when she was by herself, more than a simple climax, but real, hot human touch. His scent would surround her, his heat.

She shivered as he moved in time to the music. Nothing sexy, nothing that should send tremors of arousal through her. It was just a dry, classical piece. But Rodriguez's touch made it seem like more. It made the strains of the cello warm, made the music wind through her body, wrapping around her, as though she were a part of it. One of the instruments. And he was playing her.

She couldn't even bring herself to care, she wanted to embrace it.

This wasn't safe. This wasn't controlled. And she didn't care.

Because tonight she felt like a woman. And he was right, she had forgotten what that was like. She hadn't seen the point in remembering. It was so much safer to get lost in the world of dinners at home and imaginary games with cuddle toys.

There was nothing safe about being in Rodriguez's embrace. She'd discovered that earlier in the corridor when they'd kissed. When she'd all but attacked him, truth be told.

No, his embrace was danger. Delicious, dark, decadent, probably bad for her, but all the better for it. Part of her wondered what was wrong with her. The other part didn't care. Not now. He was stealing control out of her hands. And she was letting him.

"Feeling warm?" he asked, his voice a whisper, his lips pressed against her earlobe.

"How did you know?"

"Because I am."

"We might…step outside for a moment." *Bad idea, Carlotta. Very bad.*

"Sounds like a plan to me." A dark, glittering fire lit his eyes and she knew that it was the kind of bad idea that she'd had before, and yet, it felt different. She felt different. Not all glowy and wide-eyed, hoping for some kind of emotional revelation.

She just wanted him to touch her. Her only fear was that he wouldn't.

He kept his arm locked around her waist and she led the way through the crowd, to the back of the ballroom and out onto the vast terrace. It was warm outside, ocean mist hanging thick in the heated air.

"The beaches in Santa Christobel are famous. And I don't believe you've been yet," he said, sliding his hand over her waist and to her hand, lacing his fingers through hers.

"It's dark," she said dryly.

"This is where I say something pithy about the moon reflecting off the water. Or where I would say something to that effect if I were toying with you." He tightened his hold on her hand and halted his steps. Carlotta stopped and turned to him, studied his face, his dark eyes glittering in the dim light. "But I'm not. The simple truth is, I have wanted to have you to myself from the moment I saw you in that dress. I'm luring you away from the crowd so I can get you alone."

She sucked in a breath. "Are you planning on having your wicked way with me?" She'd meant to tease, but unfortunately her question sounded completely sincere and a little bit breathless.

"Is that what you want?"

"Why don't we go down to the beach and…see the moon."

"Sounds like a line. I should know."

She shot him her deadliest glare, one that would have sent a lesser man running for cover. But there was nothing lesser about Rodriguez. And it was dark, so her look was probably completely wasted. "Rodriguez, this isn't easy for me, can we just walk?"

"And not talk?"

"That would probably be best." She didn't want to think. She wanted…she didn't want to think about what it was she wanted either, because there was nothing smart or good or self-controlled about what she wanted. It didn't really matter if Rodriguez was the man she was supposed to marry. She didn't have any of the feelings she should have for a future husband for him, she just…needed him.

The need was elemental. It wasn't a pursuit of rebellion, it was physical. As necessary as breathing. Terrifying and foreign in its intensity, but far too compelling to walk away from.

"Then follow me." He started walking again and she followed. He led her down a stone path that went from the house and disappeared into the thick, lush sand of the beach. "You might need to lose your shoes," he said, looking down at the glittering high heels she was wearing.

"Right."

He tightened his grip on her while she lifted one foot up and toed the first spiky shoe off, then the other. He picked them up off the sand, the feminine heels out of place in his large, square hands. "I don't want you to lose them," he said.

"Thanks." She didn't really care about the shoes. She couldn't. She felt somehow outside of herself and more connected to her body's physical needs than she'd ever been. Above and also deeply immersed in what was happening to her, to them. She just wanted to block everything out but the feelings that were moving through her. The desire and lust and things she'd ignored for so long. To embrace the heat in her blood instead of trying to suppress it.

For one moment, she just wanted to be a woman. To capture what had been ripped from her life, not just by Gabriel, but by her parents and their disapproval, the media and their cruelty.

She scanned the beach, looking for a place that might afford some privacy.

"This way," he said, drawing her forward, into

a cove of palms that stood back from the water. There was a cabana there, linen curtains tied back on thick, wooden posts, blowing in the warm evening breeze.

A large, white mattress was placed in the middle on a wooden frame. It was clearly meant for two, and it was obviously meant for privacy. As private as one could get out in the open.

"Before you go and get angry, I've toured the property before. I haven't sneaked out of parties and brought dates here."

"Not here specifically."

"I never claimed to be a saint."

"Neither did I," she said, climbing the wooden steps that led into the secluded structure. "But I seem to have been trying to do an impression of one for most of my life."

She sat on the edge of the lounge and leaned back slightly, almost shocking herself with her boldness.

He approached the lounger and rested his knee on the thick, white padding, just between her thighs. He didn't touch her, but she could feel his heat, felt a hollow ache starting at her core and working its way into her stomach, making her feel needy and edgy. Nervous too.

He leaned in closer and she leaned back, the move reflexive. She could see a smile curve the corner of his wicked mouth in the dim lighting. He rested his hand next to her hip, brought his face closer to hers and she scooted back a fraction. He chuckled, resting his other palm on the other side of her so that he was over her, his lips so near her she would barely have to move to kiss him.

So she did it. She tilted her head up, bringing her mouth against his, her tongue teasing the seam. He tasted even better than she remembered. Until two weeks ago it had been so long since she'd been kissed, so long since she'd felt beautiful. So long since she'd wanted anything that was just for her.

He returned the kiss, his mouth hot and hungry, his tongue sliding against hers, the friction so sensual she thought it might kill her. She didn't think anything had ever felt so good. Her hands moved to his shoulders and she felt herself falling back slowly, her head resting against one of the throw pillows that had been placed on the lounger.

He put one hand on her leg and pushed the hem

of her dress up, allowing her to part her thighs so he could settle between them, the hard ridge of his erection hot even through layers of lace and silk, teasing her sensitized body.

He rocked against her, teasing her with the slight pressure from his arousal, pleasure pouring through her like warm oil. She arched into him, wanting more, wanting him to keep kissing her. Wanting him to touch more of her. Wanting more in general.

"Touch me," she whispered against his lips, moving her hands from his shoulders to the front of his shirt, jerking the knot on his tie, loosening it and pulling it off so she could get to the buttons on his dress shirt.

She worked the buttons quickly, desperate to touch his skin. Desperate for more. She placed her palm flat on his chest, his flesh hot and hard, the hair prickly and masculine beneath her hands.

His chest vibrated with a low, masculine growl as he tore his lips from hers and pressed a line of kisses down her neck, sucking the tender skin where it met with her shoulder. She arched her back, a silent entreaty for him to touch her breasts.

And he knew just what she wanted. He moved

his hand around to the back of her dress and with one deft motion he slid the zipper down, loosening the lacy garment so that he could tug the top down, baring her black strapless bra.

"Perfecto," he said, his palm grazing her rib cage, skimming over the tips of her breasts. Not even close to enough.

Her breath hitched, her entire body drawn so tight she thought she was going to explode. She'd never been so turned on, so fast, in her life. But she felt like she was ready to go over the edge at any moment.

He lowered his head, his tongue trailing just beneath the line of her bra, so close to what she wanted and still not enough. "Rodriguez. Please. I need more. I need you to touch me," she said, her words coming out halted, labored.

He reached his hand behind her again and undid the catch on her bra with a swift flick of his fingers. The night air was warm against her bare skin, and she couldn't feel embarrassed. Not even for a moment.

He swore, short and sharp, before lowering his head and drawing one of her nipples into his mouth. She gripped his head, lacing her fingers through his hair, holding him to her.

The heat spreading through Rodriguez was reckless. Dangerous. He enjoyed sex. Always. But it never took him over like this. Usually, the heat of desire was comparable to standing near a fireplace. Warm, something he looked forward to, but not something wild or dangerous. The feeling Carlotta gave him was more like a wildfire, burning hot, raging through him with nothing to contain it.

Her desire wasn't calm, it wasn't polite or restrained. She wanted him, and she wasn't shy about showing it. And he could give her no less. He had no ability to effect the persona of a smooth, experienced lover. Not now. He could only feel.

Her nipple hardened beneath his tongue and her obvious need for him sent a shot of pure, hard lust through him, making his erection jerk with the need to be inside her. His hands shook as he started to slide her dress down her hips. He couldn't remember trembling before sex since he was a sixteen-year-old virgin.

He felt her go stiff beneath him suddenly, her body tight when before she had been pliant in his arms. "Did you hear that?" she whispered, drawing away from him.

"No." His blood was roaring too loudly in his ears for him to hear anything.

"*Madre di dio,*" she cursed, reaching down to the side of the lounger and retrieving her bra, quickly covering her lush breasts with the band of black fabric.

"What's wrong?"

"What's wrong?" she asked, her voice nearly hysterical as she tugged the top of her dress back into place and contorted her body into an odd shape as she reached for the zipper. "Anyone could have walked up here, that's what's wrong!" she hissed.

"Do you need help?" he asked, indicating her struggle with the zipper, his brain still moving slowly.

"Yes," she said, turning, her face angled down. "I thought I heard someone."

"I don't hear anyone."

"That isn't the point."

He tugged the zipper into place and she turned. "What is the point then?" he asked.

"That we could have been caught."

"So what? We're engaged."

"So?" she choked out, her words rising as she stood from the lounger. "So? You clearly have never been the center of a tabloid scandal. Oh, yes, you have, you just don't care! Well, I care!"

"Carlotta, there wasn't anyone out here. And anyway, we're engaged to be married, where's the scandal?"

"Where's the scandal? You can hardly find pictures of royals kissing each other politely, let alone…snogging…in a cabana!"

"We were a little bit past that point."

"Don't," she said, her voice trembling as she bent down and grabbed his tie, tossed it in his direction, "remind me."

"Why are you so angry? Nothing happened. There were no pictures."

"But there could have been!" she said. "And they would have been online and my…my son would have seen them. It's bad enough that Luca will be able to look his family up on the internet, see that they called him the Santina bastard. See the endless speculation about who his father is, the headlines intimating *I* might not know who it is. Should he also see pictures of me half naked on a lounge chair with a man?"

"No, I don't suppose he should but I am the man you're marrying."

"You keep saying that like it matters. It doesn't matter. What matters is that I… How can you understand? You just…can't."

"Try me, Carlotta. Do you think you have the monopoly on whatever it is you're feeling right now?"

"On this? Yes. I'm sure I do. At least when it comes to the two of us."

"I didn't think you were a saint. You're doing a great impression of someone who finds themself to be holier than thou."

"I *want* to be," she said sharply. "I want to be better than this. I need to be." Her voice broke on the last word, the desperation he heard there something he couldn't understand. Something he didn't think he wanted to understand.

"Better than what? People want sex, Carlotta. They need it. It's fundamental. A drive, like eating and sleeping. It's not wrong to want it."

"You say that because you have no idea what it means to face the consequences of it. It's not the same as eating and sleeping. You have to be careful. And I should be in control of myself…of my body. I should have control."

She turned and walked away, her arms crossed over her front like she was cold, holding on to herself tightly. He didn't follow her. She didn't want him to. He knew it. He wanted to. He wanted to find out what her problem was. To figure out why her rejection of him made his stomach feel tight, his body numb. It was more than unquenched desire. More than simple disappointment over not achieving a climax.

He wasn't sure what it was.

He watched her small figure until she made her way back up to the expansive home and slipped back into the ballroom. He hoped she didn't attract attention.

Not for his sake. For hers. Because she hated having her photo taken.

He couldn't remember the last time the needs of someone else seemed so much more important than his own.

CHAPTER SEVEN

CARLOTTA closed the door to Luca's room silently, her heart heavy. With responsibility. Anguish. Guilt. Nothing was ever simple.

She'd made a hasty retreat through the less populated portion of the mansion, and had managed not to run into anyone beyond a few members of staff. A trick she'd learned during her last idiotic affair.

That thought made her feel sick. Why was she still struggling like this? Why, when she knew the kind of pain it could cause, had she let her guard down?

The easy answer was that Rodriguez and her need for him had blindsided her. She liked sex, and yes, she'd missed it periodically over the past six years, but the need for completion had never, ever been like it had been tonight with Rodriguez.

This was just plain scary. Shocking in its intensity. It was taking her over.

She was tempted to go back in Luca's room and curl up with her sleeping son. Use him as a shield against everything Rodriguez had conjured up in her. Yes, he had reminded her that she was a woman, not simply a mother, a caregiver. But someone with needs of her own.

And she wished she hadn't been given that reminder.

She leaned back against Luca's bedroom doors and closed her eyes. And she gave in to the misery that was making her entire body feel too tight. She let one tear slide down her cheek, then another. A sharp, silent sob forced her to suck in a breath.

"*Dios*. Are you okay?"

She turned toward the sound of Rodriguez's voice, wiping away the moisture on her face, hoping he didn't notice that her hands were shaking. "F-fine, I'm fine."

"Luca?"

"Sleeping. I'm just..."

"I didn't hurt you, did I?" He took a step toward her, his dark brows locked together. "I thought... you seemed to want everything..."

"I did," she whispered.

"Did someone hurt you? Did Luca's father..."

She laughed, the sound hollow and watery. Pitiful. "Yes. Of course he did. We aren't together as one big happy family, are we? But he didn't… hurt me…not like you mean."

He looked over his shoulder, down the long corridor, vacant for now, but they both knew that staff were still milling around, even though it was past midnight.

"Come on," he said, touching her hand lightly. "Come talk to me."

She followed him, trying desperately to keep from dissolving into a dribbly mess. Because no one had really wanted to talk to her about what had happened. Not with any real depth or meaning.

Come talk to me.

The way he said it was like he really wanted to hear it. But she wasn't sure she could tell. Not when it seemed to live inside her, a dirty secret that roamed around in her belly like a hungry lion, consuming happiness, her joy in normal things. Reminding her, constantly, that she'd failed. That she could never be worthy of forgiveness.

He pushed open wide, double doors at the end of the corridor. His room, she knew. And yet, even though a couple of days ago she might have accused him of trying to seduce her, she didn't think that tonight.

Anyway, she'd practically led the seducing earlier.

The front section of his chamber was a sitting area, and that seemed neutral enough. She sat in one of the chairs, the one farthest from any of the other chairs, because if they were going to have this discussion, she was keeping her distance. Keeping her control.

Rodriguez didn't sit. He stood, leaning against the mantel, his posture relaxed, arms folded across his broad chest. He'd never put his tie back on and the top few buttons of his shirt were still open.

From her clawing at them like a deranged sex kitten.

Che cavolo.

"I'm sorry," she said tightly.

"Why?"

"The whole thing is…all of this. You were supposed to marry Sophia—"

"I was never particularly attracted to Sophia," he said, his voice rough.

"But Sophia wouldn't have… I guess it doesn't really matter."

"Carlotta, I get that you don't want to be the focus of tabloids and Luca does make things different. I know you're worried about him seeing things that have been written about you when he's old enough to look for them. Honestly, I had never given a thought to what any children of mine might think if they saw the stories written about me. I understand it now. But nothing happened tonight and…"

"Tonight," she said, choosing her words carefully, "proved that I haven't changed. I thought I had control over myself."

"So you said earlier, but I still don't get it. Chasing a little sexual pleasure, I don't see the harm in it."

"You wouldn't. But I know the other side of it, don't I? I know what happens when you let something have control over you." She drew in a shaky breath, her stomach tightening. "Everything seemed so perfect when I met him. I'd never met a man that I really wanted before. But everything he said sounded so nice, and everything he did felt so good. For a girl who had held on to her virginity for as long as I did, I think his seduction time was record breaking. For a few stolen weekends it was great. Gabriel was—is—a political ambassador that my family was working quite closely with at the time. Every time he came to the palace I would sneak out of my room to be with him."

"Carlotta, if you think you're the first girl to be seduced by the kind of man that makes promises but only wants sex, you're wrong. There are a lot of men gifted in saying just the right things, or the wrong things, to get a woman into bed. But that's his sin, not yours."

She laughed. "If that were the whole story, sure. I might believe you. I asked him one night, could we take things public. I was ready. Ready to marry him, or just live with him, whatever he would give me. But I wanted to spend the whole night with him, not sneak back to my room after he was finished with me. And that was when I found out about Kristen. She's Gabriel's wife of fifteen years. They have four children. And when he was away on important business trips, supposedly working, he was sleeping with me." Her voice broke.

"Carlotta…" he said, taking a step toward her.

"Don't. You have to hear the rest. I was…utterly heartbroken. Completely. And that was when I… This is what I can't forgive myself for, Rodriguez. I can't." For a moment, she couldn't speak, her voice buried beneath the pressure in her chest, the shame, the guilt. She was sick with it, heavy. She felt too tired to go on, and yet, she couldn't stop. She had to tell him. Had to let it out.

She swallowed hard. "He…he wanted me again. He wanted to still be with me." Her voice shook but she continued anyway. "He told me he loved me. And I believed him. And that night, I let myself forget about Kristen, just for a few moments. I let him have me one more time. Because I wasn't ready to let him go. Because for one, stupid moment, I believed him when he said we could find a way to make it work."

She choked on the admission, her skin crawling even as she confessed it out loud. "I can't scrub that night off my skin, Rodriguez. Not after six years." A sob assaulted her. "And tonight I proved that I haven't changed."

That was the part that no one knew. Something she'd never been able to speak out loud. The part that made it impossible to let it all go. She had been stupid enough, going into a clandestine, purely sexual affair with a man that she didn't really know. But trying to block out the full horror of reality when she'd heard it from his own lips? When she'd known, known his wife was at home, in their bed alone, and he was with Carlotta.

That was something she hated herself for. That she hadn't been able to stop loving him in that instant. That she had given in when she'd had a chance to turn back.

"The only real consolation of that is, by my dates, I was already pregnant. At least that last time…and it's hard to even talk about because the one thing, the only thing, I don't regret from that affair was Luca. But if I had gotten pregnant from that time, when I knew he was married… that would have been much harder to handle."

Rodriguez didn't speak, he only looked at her, his eyes unreadable, black bottomless pools, in the dim lamplight of the sitting area. He stood frozen and for one, horrible moment she was afraid he was just going to turn around and leave her there.

Then he moved to her, crouching down in front of her, clasping her hands in his.

"That man was a bastard. He took advantage of

you, of the fact that you loved him. He cheated both you, and his wife. All of his children. He should carry the shame of this, and I'm willing to bet that he doesn't."

She forced a laugh. "I'm sure he doesn't. I'm sure he doesn't care enough about either of us."

He moved his thumb over the back of her hand. "What happened? After he told you, after the last time you were together?"

He kept holding on to her, offering her strength. She looked down at their hands, joined together in her lap. "I had to find my clothes. I gathered them up, and I went into the bathroom. Then I threw up."

It had been awful, her entire body shaking and then, with Gabriel watching from the bed, she'd had to stumble from the room, be sick right in bathroom, where he could hear. Where he would know just how much pain she was in.

"And then I got dressed, and I walked out. I avoided him the next day and prayed he wouldn't come back again. I started feeling sick soon after that and then I realized…and I had to tell my father. Everything. He made me tell Gabriel. And then he paid Gabriel a lot of money. To never come back. To keep quiet when the media discovered I was pregnant."

She breathed in deeply. "It wasn't like in movies where a woman finds out she's pregnant and it's somehow this wonderful moment. I was horrified. Numb. I had to go to the doctor and get tested for every STD under the sun because clearly our birth control efforts had failed, and there was no telling who else he'd been sleeping with. What he might have given me. And I just sort of existed for the next few months. I didn't want to feel the baby kick. It made it too real. But when Luca was born...that was like the movies. He was just so tiny and vulnerable. And he needed me. But I realized then how much I needed him too. He gave me purpose. He made me want to be better."

"And better is denying you have sexual desire?" he asked, his voice soft.

"That's what it's meant since Gabriel, yes. But it's not just that. It's everything. Things that feel good can be wrong. You have to trust in something more than feelings."

"He was a bastard."

"For cheating on his wife? Don't you plan on cheating on me?"

Rodriguez looked down at Carlotta, at her face, streaked with tears he wasn't even certain she'd noticed. The confession had cost her, and he could well understand why. And now, faced with her question, he felt like he'd been eviscerated by her words.

Yes. He had been planning on carrying on as he'd always done. But he had promised honesty. Surely that changed things? Now though, he didn't feel like it did.

"I promised you honesty," he said, his voice rough.

She nodded. "I know."

"I won't hurt you."

"Rodriguez…"

"I am not the same as he is." He said it to convince himself, and the sad part was, he didn't feel convinced. Not even remotely. He felt like he was deserving of every ounce of scorn he was ready to heap onto the man who had dared play with Carlotta in that way. Who had taken a young woman's fragile emotions and used them so he could find satisfaction in her body.

And for the first time he wondered how he was different than a man like that. Because he had always assumed his behavior was fine. He always parted with his partners on good terms. They had fun, in bed and out, he bought them gifts, he made them feel good about themselves. He'd never considered it wrong, not for a moment.

Now he wondered if he had ever left a woman feeling like that. If he'd truly only used his lovers.

No, he'd never been guilty of quite what Gabriel had. No children, no cheating.

But he had been planning on doing that. To Carlotta. To Luca. It would have been in the tabloids. Luca would be able to see it.

"I won't cheat," he said, the words falling from his lips before he had a chance to think them through.

"What?"

"I will stay faithful to you. If you will do the same for me."

"Forever?"

"Forever. I can't promise any deep, abiding emotion I...I can't." It was the honest truth, a limitation of his that he had accepted long ago. Embraced. "I just don't have that. But I can control my actions, and I never want to put you in the position of being hurt or humiliated again. I will never do to you what Gabriel did to his wife. And I don't want Luca seeing tabloid photos of me out with other women."

He had never believed he had it in him to be a good father. He still didn't. He knew nothing about it. The mere thought of his own father made him feel ill. But he wouldn't flaunt any kind of disrespect for Luca's mother. Wouldn't have Luca seeing evidence of infidelity in their marriage.

If Rodriguez had had a mother he could remember, he would have wanted the same.

And he didn't want to be anything like the man who was Luca's father in genes only.

She looked up at him, her green eyes rimmed in red from crying. "I promise to be faithful to you too."

He felt like they were taking vows now. Like everything spoken between them in this room would be binding.

"I need you to promise something else too," he said.

"What's that?" she asked, her voice a whisper.

"Gabriel's not invited into our bed."

She grimaced. "No problem."

"I don't mean literally, and I don't mean in the

sense that I think you might fantasize about him or something. I mean any hang-ups he's left you with. The guilt. You loved him. It didn't just go away when he admitted he'd lied to you. I've never loved anyone, Carlotta. I know it makes people do things they wouldn't normally do. And I just want you."

She drew in a shaking breath. "I don't know if I can, Rodriguez. What I did was...I can't forgive myself for it."

"How long did your affair with him last?"

"Every weekend for about eight weeks."

"And you fell in love with him?"

"I was a twenty-three-year-old virgin. I thought I was in love with him the moment I went to bed with him, the night that I met him. I saw white dresses and diamond rings and forever."

"And if you had known he was married when you met, what would you have done?"

"I never would have let him touch me."

"He waited to tell you until he knew he had you wrapped around his finger. He's the one who should be ashamed. Deeply. He deceived you. He manipulated you."

"I still did the wrong thing," she insisted.

"And I am in no position to throw stones. I've made mistakes. That's another thing I'll never ask of you. I'll never ask you to be perfect, because I know I never will be."

"I think I can do that," she said, her voice trembling, a small laugh escaping.

"I know this isn't what either of us expected, but I think we can make it work." He moved his thumb over her smooth, creamy skin. His body responding to the silken texture, to her scent. Even now, he could remember how it had been to caress the even softer skin of her breasts. A tremor of lust rocked him.

"And you'll always tell the truth?"

"I will," he said.

"What are you thinking right now?"

He gritted his teeth. "I'm thinking about how much I want to continue what we started on the beach. How beautiful your breasts are. How much I want to taste them again."

Her cheeks flushed deep rose, her full lips curving up slightly. "Not exactly what I was expecting."

"But honest," he said.

"I want you too, but…"

"Forget everything right now. What do you want?"

"You," she said. "I want to make love with you. But…"

He leaned in and kissed her. Carlotta closed her eyes and let the touch of Rodriguez's mouth on her wash everything away. The guilt. The hurt. His kiss cleansed her, left her empty, wanting, then filled her again with desire, need.

She'd told him the truth and he still wanted her. Maybe she could do this after all. Want it. Want him.

She'd had her guilt tangled up in desire for so long. Had seen desire as her downfall. Not just sexual desire, but the wild part of herself she was afraid was always beneath the surface. She'd let a part of it out before, but Rodriguez, wanting him, made it flood her. She felt out of control, but in the very best way. What would happen if she gave in? Not on their wedding night, not when it was expected, but now. When it was her choice.

To follow her desire and prove to herself that she could have sex and pleasure, like a normal woman. To prove that she didn't have to spend her whole life being punished for one mistake.

She wanted to believe it. She wanted so much for Rodriguez's words to be true. She wanted to accept forgiveness. So badly she ached with the need of it.

"Yes, Rodriguez, please," she said against his lips. "Please make love with me." A rush of relief flooded her when she spoke the words. Like invisible bonds had broken and she was free. To feel, fully and completely, the need that he inspired in her. To want him as a woman wanted a man without the ghost of her past mistakes haunting her. Without inhibition. Without the cloying, crushing weight of expectation that had been on her all of her life.

She'd never felt anything like this before. She was immersed in sexual desire, in reckless need. There was no thought. No control.

His kiss deepened, intensified, and she returned it, her tongue delving deeply into his mouth, the feeling sending a thrill of pleasure through her, making her body ache for more.

He unzipped her dress quickly and she helped by unhooking her bra and letting it fall to the floor. She was eager to get back where they had been. To take what she'd denied herself earlier.

He didn't disappoint. Rodriguez lowered his head, tracing the valley between her breasts with the tip of his tongue. She shivered at the contact, her nipples tightening along with an answering clenching of the muscles low in her stomach.

His tongue edged nearer to her nipple and she held her breath, waiting for him to give her more. To give her what she wanted. He didn't. And it wasn't because he didn't know. His low, husky chuckle told her he knew exactly what he was doing to her. And that he was doing it on purpose.

"Rodriguez." She panted his name, not caring if she sounded like she was begging. Because she was.

She arched into him, and he honored the request, drawing one tightened bud deep into his mouth, the suction resonating within her, deep and low, making her internal muscles clench tight. He turned his attention to her other breast, and she let her head fall back, reveling in his attention, allowing herself to feel every sensation that was firing through her bloodstream.

He moved his head away and blew lightly on her damp skin, the shock of cold air tightening the bonds of arousal around her body, holding her captive to need.

She gripped the back of his head, her fingers wound tightly in his hair, every muscle in her body tensing, waiting to find out what he would do next. He kissed her, just beneath her breasts, then again lower, tracing a line to her belly button with the tip of his tongue before he gripped the bunched-up sides of her gown and tugged it down her legs.

"Still good, *querida*?" he asked, his voice rough.

"Yes," she breathed. "So good."

"It will only get better." He pulled her panties down her legs and parted them gently, his tongue gliding along her inner thigh.

Her entire body was trembling, nerves and arousal making her stomach churn. He traced the line of her delicate flesh, his tongue delving between her slick folds. A hoarse sound escaped her lips as she gripped his shoulders, trying to keep herself from jumping away from him. Making sure he didn't abandon her.

The sensations, the intensity of them, were almost too much. He continued to pleasure her with long strokes of his tongue and she felt like she was going to shatter and fall into a million pieces all around him.

When he pushed one finger inside her, she did. An explosion of pleasure roared through her, her core pulsing around him as he worked to draw her climax out to impossible heights, impossible lengths.

She felt weak after, spent, but far from finished.

He wrapped his arms around her and drew her down onto the floor with him, then holding her tightly to his chest, he stood and began to walk into the bedroom area of his chamber. She'd never been carried by anyone, not since she was a child. He made her feel feminine. Cherished.

And it made warm and fuzzy feelings start growing in her. That was bad. She didn't want warm and fuzzy. She wanted hot and lusty. She managed to push past the post-orgasm languor and focus on how much she wanted him. All of him. In her. With her.

He set her on the edge of the bed and quickly stripped off his shirt and went to work on his pants, kicking off his shoes and socks, tugging his underwear down with the slacks and pushing them all to the side.

He was so much hotter than she'd even imagined. His muscles sharp, hard cut and deliciously defined, with just the right amount of dark hair over gorgeous olive skin. And when she looked down past his chest, and his impressive length, her whole body went liquid with desire.

She leaned forward to take her shoes off.

"No," he said. "Leave them."

She straightened and pushed herself backward so that her entire body was on the bed, and, never taking her eyes off his, she leaned back, her high-heel-clad feet flat on the bedspread, her entire body open and bare for him.

It was a little bit frightening, and also liberating, to offer herself to him, to see the stark desire in his handsome face.

"Remind me to drop the maharaja a thank-you note," he said, his words tight.

"Why?" she whispered.

"Because I'm very thankful he ran off with Sophia. If he hadn't, I wouldn't be in this moment. And I don't think I have ever wanted another woman the way I want you."

She shifted and rose up on her knees, coming back over to the edge of the bed. She gripped the hard length of his arousal and squeezed him, watching as his expression changed, as his control slipped.

She leaned in and circled the head of his erection with her tongue and a harsh sound escaped his lips. He pulled away from her, his chest rising and falling heavily. "Not yet," he said. "Not like that."

He leaned over and opened the drawer on his side table, pulling out a condom packet. She took it from his hand and tore it open, rolling it onto him surprisingly fast given how badly her hands were still shaking. From her semi-release, from her continued arousal, from nerves, excitement and just about every other feeling she could think of.

He joined her on the bed and she thought her heart was going to climb up her throat. He was sexy, and big, and amazing, and big, and she hoped everything still worked like it was supposed to.

"Relax," he said, drawing her to him, her naked breasts pressing tightly against his chest, the crisp hair there stimulating her nipples, making her stomach tighten, her internal muscles pulse.

He cupped her bottom with one large hand and lay back, bringing her with him, so that she was halfway on top of him. He kissed her, his touching helping to banish the sudden onslaught of nerves.

She shifted and brought the head of his erection up against the slick entrance of her body. He brought both of his hands to her hips, holding her tightly as she slid down onto his length. She couldn't hold back the sound of satisfaction as he filled her, stretched her.

"Oh, yes," she whispered, rising up again, then down, learning the right rhythm for both of them.

His grip tightened on her, one hand staying firm on her hip, the other moving over her breasts, teasing her nipples as she rode him.

When her orgasm hit, she leaned forward and braced her hand on his shoulder, holding herself still as wave after wave of pleasure washed over her, her breath coming in short, sharp bursts. He wrapped his arms around her and switched their positions, thrusting hard into her as he sought his own release. She moved against him, each one of his thrusts bringing her closer, impossibly, to another climax.

When she reached the edge this time, they went

over together, his harsh growl of completion the final component that brought her to the brink.

They lay together, sweat-slicked limbs entwined, the only sound in the room their harsh breathing.

She'd had sex with Rodriguez. Because she'd wanted to. Because she'd wanted him. She had let go. Of everything. Of her control. She had let it all drop and she had simply been Carlotta. Not the woman she was supposed to be. Just the woman she was.

And the world hadn't crumbled. Quite the opposite. Things seemed right for the first time. She didn't feel like she was being suffocated in her own body, crushed beneath the weight, the expectation, that she would be able to be a perfect kind of superwoman.

With Rodriguez, she had simply been herself.

A tear slid down her cheek and landed on his chest. She felt free.

CHAPTER EIGHT

SEX was always good for Rodriguez. It was something he'd used, from a very early age, to escape from the world. To get lost in feelings that were purely good, so that he could block out a recent beating he'd received from his father's hand, or a verbal assault that had flayed him from the inside out.

But sex was never like this. It had never been about giving with no thought to what he might get back. Though Carlotta had given back more than he'd ever experienced before, it hadn't been his primary objective.

It hadn't even entered his mind.

Their bodies had simply worked together. The give and take so perfect and rewarding. He had been lost in her. In the touch of her hands, her taste, her scent. He could have lavished her with attention all night and not been satisfied. Not wholly.

That was another new and unique aspect. This sort of strange, bone-deep fulfillment that made him feel both sated and in need of more.

But not now. Now Carlotta was wrapped around him, her breath deep, warm and moist across his chest.

And he didn't feel trapped, or crowded, or anything he'd thought he might feel sleeping in the same bed with a woman.

He'd never, ever slept with a lover in the pure, literal sense of the word.

He was up and gone after sex. It was just the sort of liaison he conducted, the kind he was comfortable with. And he made sure he pursued women who wanted the same sort of arrangement.

He didn't want anyone in his life, only between the sheets. He'd managed to make it to twenty-nine without ever sharing a bed with a woman for the express purpose of what a bed had been built for.

He liked it. The warm weight of her on his chest, liked stroking his hand over her sleek, dark hair. And really enjoyed taking advantage of running his other hand over her bare curves, her skin silken beneath his fingertips.

Carlotta's body jerked and she pushed herself up partway. "Oh!"

"Are you okay?" he asked.

"Mmm," she whimpered, putting her hand over her face and scrubbing at it for a moment. "What time is it?"

He craned his neck behind them. "Six-thirty." And he hadn't slept at all. He'd simply lain there, dissecting the events of the night, enjoying being with her.

"Oh, no," she said, moving into a sitting position. "Luca will be up in a bit."

"Let Angelina get him."

"He comes in looking for me sometimes," she said, her voice thick from sleep. "I need to go back to my room."

A strange flash of something sharp and hot stabbed him in the gut. Was he jealous of a five-year-old? Impossible. And ridiculous.

Why was he arguing? He didn't need to sleep with her. They'd had sex. And that was what having a woman in his bed was all about. Yes, it had been nice to have her with him, but there was no reason for it to feel *essential* that she stay.

But he sat up with her, unwilling to lie back

down if she was getting up. He stood and kicked his clothes, still bunched up by the bed, to the side. Carlotta's eyes were glued to him in the dim light.

"See something you like?" he asked, walking over to his dresser and digging until he produced a soft black T-shirt.

"A lot of something I like," she said softly.

He threw the shirt to her and she caught it. "So you don't have to walk back down the hall in an evening gown," he said.

"Is anyone up?"

"Possibly. But trust me, you in the hall in something you might have slept in is less of a scandal than you roaming around in the previous night's attire."

"Yeah, that's true." She didn't make a move to put it on, she just sat there, holding the soft cotton top over her breasts. He wished she wouldn't cover them up.

He wasn't used to this. This strange kind of tense emotion hanging in the air after sex. Sex was supposed to be a release but he felt...fuller somehow. Satisfied yet...yet in desperate need of more. As though he'd tapped into a hunger he

didn't know he possessed, and now that he'd un-
covered it, he was almost certain he would never
be able to fill it.

He took a deep breath and tried to ease the tight
sensation in his chest.

"Are you all right?" he asked, another thing he'd
never been compelled to ask after being with a
woman. It was all usually clean and focused. It
was about the physical, for him and his partner,
nothing more.

But Carlotta was going to be his wife. And there
was nothing clean and simple about permanent.
Or about what she'd told him. About the issues
that she had.

Just thinking about that man, Gabriel, was
enough to choke him. The bastard had taken something he had no right to. He had stolen Carlotta's
love of herself.

"Yeah," she said, not quite meeting his gaze.
"I'm good."

"You're beautiful," he said. Always when he
said it to her, something he'd said easily to so
many other women, it felt different. It felt real
and essential. It felt like something he had to tell
her. Something he had to make her understand.

"Thank you." She tugged the shirt on, and he watched, savoring every visible inch of her until she was covered.

"You don't really seem like you believe me."

"I'm not sure that it matters."

"Why not?"

"We're sort of stuck with each other, right?"

He frowned. "It matters because it's true. And because I don't feel stuck." That was true. He wasn't sure when that feeling had changed, and why it had changed after his promise to be faithful. If anything, the specter of a lifetime of sleeping with the same woman should be looming over him and taunting him with the hellish reality that such prolonged fidelity would bring.

But it wasn't. And he didn't feel any kind of dawning horror creeping over him. Right now, the only thing the thought of a lifetime of Carlotta in his bed brought was an intense, hard kick of lust.

"You don't?"

"I didn't promise to be faithful to you just to get you into bed. I promised it because I knew it was one I could keep, one I don't mind keeping."

"Hmm," she said, standing from the bed. "It's just a strange way of putting it."

"What do you want me to say? I'm trying to tell you, you're beautiful."

"I know, I just…Rodriguez I don't know what I'm doing. I… Thank you. Thank you for not wanting to cheat on me, and for thinking I'm beautiful."

"That makes it not sound very spectacular."

"It actually is. I wish you understood how much. Because I believe you."

His heart squeezed tight. "I think I understand."

She smiled. "Good. I'm going to go now and make sure Luca's all right."

Carlotta edged out of the bedroom and closed the door gently behind her, trying to ignore the dizzy feeling that was making her feel imbalanced and wobbly. She leaned against the wall and fought the urge to collapse. To cry. To scream, maybe.

She felt scared and excited. Hopeful in a way.

She felt like she had a piece of herself back. Or like she'd found herself for the first time. Like she'd punched a hole in the outer shell she'd built around herself from the time she was a child. Like she was ready to emerge from it fully, completely.

Now all she had to do was remember that the

sex might feel good. Great. Amazing. But that didn't mean Rodriguez was going to confess his undying love for her. Just that right now it was good. And she believed him when he said he'd be faithful. To a point.

The one thing she believed, wholly and absolutely, was that he couldn't give love. It was that blank void she kept glimpsing, the bottomless pit of emptiness she could see in his eyes.

And when she thought of him, she needed to remember that, and not simply the way he'd looked at her when she'd told him her secret. With shock, and anger, not at her but directed at Gabriel, and with nothing but compassion and caring for her.

Even Natalia, her wilder half, had looked at her in openmouthed shock when she'd started to tell her about Gabriel. About his double life. It was why she'd only *started* talking about him, and never finished the whole story.

Not until last night.

She was very glad she'd waited now. Because even if she and Rodriguez would never love each other, they understood each other.

And that was something rare. Nonexistent in her life. Sophia was the closest thing she had to a confidante anymore and, even then, she hadn't ever felt like she could really tell her everything.

But Rodriquez had stripped her bare. And she'd liked it.

A smile curved her lips even as a tear slid down her cheek. Now she just had to remember about the falling in love part and everything might go just fine.

She pushed off from the wall and headed to Luca's room, ignoring the small sliver of pain that lodged itself in her heart.

"Good morning."

Rodriguez walked into the dining room and was treated to a wide smile from a very perky Luca, who was dipping a churro in his hot chocolate, and a very shy smile from Carlotta, her cheeks glowing pink as she lifted her coffee cup to her lips.

"Morning," she said softly.

He wanted to kiss her, but he wasn't sure if he should. He'd never really worried about that. Not for a long time. He'd started flaunting his behavior the moment he'd outgrown his father. Just about daring the old man to try something with him when they were matched for strength.

But right now, it mattered. Because Carlotta was different from other women. Because he didn't want to do something wrong in front of Luca.

What she'd said about him seeing pictures... it weighed on him. His father hadn't been an example for him. His father had been the iron fist, in charge of his kingdom, but even more, ruler of his own household.

Rodriguez had started life desperate to stay in line. He had ended up doing just the opposite. Creating scandal for the sake of it.

But now Luca would see that. As would the child he and Carlotta would eventually have. The heir. It was all a lot heavier than the thoughts he was used to dwelling on.

And it kept him from kissing her.

"Sleep well?" he asked, unable to keep the intimate note from his tone.

"Uh, yeah," she said, looking sideways at Luca.

"I had a bad dream," Luca said, applying the question about sleep to himself, clearly.

Rodriguez hesitated, never quite sure how to talk to him. "You did?"

"Yes. It was about lions."

"Lions?"

"Why..." He looked at Carlotta, who seemed fine letting him handle it. "Why lions?"

"They bite," Luca returned, deadly serious.

"I don't think you have anything to worry about, as far as lions go," he said.

"I did in my dream," Luca said, his expression completely serious.

"Dreams aren't real, Luca," Carlotta said, her tone full of warmth.

Rodriguez liked that she talked to Luca. That she never got angry with him for saying what was on his mind. But it made him remember. Dinners that lasted for hours where he was expected to sit and be the heir. Being the heir meant being an object, a collector's item of interest his father might show dignitaries. Somewhere between his collection of pistols and his prize Andalusians.

He remembered being maybe Luca's age, sitting here, too afraid to move or speak. Sitting in a dining chair at this same table, wearing a tie that felt like it was choking him. Knowing that if he moved or spoke he would be punished severely. Which meant his options were to sit and try to listen. Never fall asleep. He'd done that once and the resulting punishment had been enough to make sure he'd never done it again.

The idea of someone treating Luca that way, of someone making him stand without moving for hours, smacking his shins if he dared try anything…it made his blood burn.

"You don't have to be afraid, Luca," he said, his voice hoarse. "Of lions," he finished, not sure why he'd spoken the words out loud. "There are no lions in Santa Christobel. None anywhere near here, except at the zoo. We can…go to the zoo if you like. And you can see some lions. They'll be behind fences though."

Luca eyed him skeptically, his expression so like Carlotta's it was uncanny. "They won't be able to get out?"

"No," he said, slowly realizing that, whatever he'd had planned today, he was going to the zoo instead.

"Then that sounds good. Are you coming, Mama?"

Carlotta's lips curved into a half-smile and she flicked him a glance. "Of course."

* * *

A trip to the zoo with Rodriguez wasn't an average trip to the zoo. It involved having overnight bags packed, and a quick ride on his private jet from Santa Christobel to Barcelona.

Luca was captivated by the zoo from the moment they walked in, and he didn't seem to notice the covert security detail that created a people-free bubble around them while they traversed the paths that wound through the park.

Every section of the park had been landscaped with plants native to the environment of the animals, the enclosures made as minimal as possible, everything man-made blending into the background, as much as possible.

"This is lovely, Rodriguez. Did you come here as a boy?" she asked, watching Luca's eyes go round with delight as they came to an exhibit with two tawny owls.

"Like Sherbie and Sherbet!" he said, running up to the front of their Plexiglas enclosure.

"Yes, darling," she said, laughing at his enthusiasm.

"I've never been to the zoo before," Rodriguez said, his eyes trained on the owls.

"Never? How is that...?"

He shrugged. "We didn't do things like this when I was a boy. And when I was older...I was more interested in women than owls."

"I see." She watched the back of Luca's head, seeing the sun shine on his glossy, dark hair. She suddenly wanted to pull him to her. To hold him close.

She looked at the man standing next to her. She wanted to hold him too. He should have been taken to the zoo.

"Well, we're here now," she said, moving closer to him, but not touching him.

"There's a woman here too. A beautiful one. So clearly I didn't know what I was talking about," he said, offering her one of his lady-slaying grins. It was the first concession he'd made to any kind of attraction all day. It also rang a bit false.

Not because she doubted his attraction, not possible after last night, but because the easy flirty thing wasn't as easy and flirty today as it was sometimes. Or maybe it really never was that easy and she just knew him better now.

"I like those owls!" Luca said, turning and treating them both to a big smile.

Rodriguez let out a short laugh at that and it

made a warm spot start in Carlotta's heart and spread outward. That wasn't a sexual feeling either. It was decidedly fuzzy, and directed at Rodriguez. That wasn't good.

She cleared her throat. "Ready to go see something else, Luca?"

Luca frowned. "The lions, I guess."

"You guess?" she asked.

He took a deep breath, his small shoulders rising dramatically. "I'm ready." He looked up at Rodriguez and stuck out his hand.

Rodriguez looked down at the small, outstretched hand and he felt something akin to panic well up in him. He swallowed hard, and looked into earnest green eyes, then up into Carlotta's matching green eyes. And he couldn't hurt either of them by denying Luca's nonverbal request.

He reached out and wrapped his hand around Luca's tiny fingers. He felt small. Fragile. And it reminded him, so vividly, what it was like to be that size. So powerless. And yet, for the first time, it also made him understand what it was to truly want to protect someone.

"Do you have the map, Carlotta?" he asked, his throat tight.

"Yes. For lions, we keep going straight."

"All right then." He tightened his grip on Luca's hand and walked down the cobblestone trail, Luca's legs having to take two steps to his one. He slowed down to try and match the boy's pace and Carlotta moved next to Luca, taking his other hand in hers.

It was a scene of domesticity he'd never quite imagined being a part of. Not as a child, not as… whatever he was to Luca. A stepfather, or at least future stepfather. Strange to think of himself that way. Strange to have Luca cling to him as though Rodriguez was going to offer him protection.

He looked over Luca's head at Carlotta. She could have made Luca the sort of child who didn't trust people. She had ample reason to. But it was clear that Luca simply accepted that anyone his mother deemed all right was trustworthy.

Already, Luca accepted that he was safe with him and that was… It was humbling in a way he had not anticipated. And still created that bit of panic in him.

"There they are," he said, pointing to the enclosure. There were four lions lounging by the tall fence, and he felt Luca shrink by his side, his little body tense. "We can go if you like," he said. "We don't have to stay." Because more than anything, he didn't want to lose Luca's trust.

When he thought of what his own father would have done in this situation, it made his entire body want to recoil. "I'll look at them," Luca said, his grip tightening on Rodriguez's hand. He stood stiff next to Rodriguez, his eyes fixed on the lions.

"They aren't bad, Luca. See?" he said.

The large golden creatures were lethargic in the midday heat, stretched out by the fence, ears twitching. They didn't seem to notice, or care, that they were being watched.

Gradually, Luca relaxed, but he never released his hold on Rodriguez. "We can go now," Luca said.

Rodriguez laughed and looked at Carlotta. "I'm sure that's fine."

The smile Carlotta gave him was something new too. There was trust there. A different kind than the kind she'd shown him last night. Something that seemed even bigger.

"Lead the way, Luca," Carlotta said, still holding her son's hand.

Luca didn't release his hold on Rodriguez, so

he continued on with them, letting Luca cling to him like he was a lifeline, and wondering what the little boy would think if he knew what kind of man Rodriguez really was.

"He's completely exhausted," Carlotta said, closing the door to the bedroom she'd installed Luca in. He had been placed, strategically, on the opposite end of the penthouse to this room, and the room Carlotta had installed herself in.

Angelina's room was next to Luca's, and she was ready to take care of him during the night. He hoped that would entice Carlotta to come to his bed. And stay in it all night.

Angelina had spent the day in Barcelona and had returned late, arms full of shopping bags, ready to stay at the penthouse with Luca, so he could take Carlotta out for the evening.

"I'm not surprised he's tired. I can't even guess how much ground we covered today."

"We kept having to run back and see the lions," she said, a smile curving her full lips. He hadn't touched her all day, hadn't thought he should with Luca there. Now he was aching with the need to pull her into his arms.

To feel her soft, naked body against his.

She'd made him wait two weeks after the explosive kiss in the hall to finally satisfy his desire for her. He'd never waited for a woman before. They'd been interchangeable. Carlotta was not. Carlotta felt necessary.

And after having her once, he only needed her more.

Rodriguez forced a laugh through his constricted throat. "Here's hoping we don't have a nightmare relapse as a result."

"I doubt it. He'll be sleeping too soundly. I love the penthouse, by the way," she said, indicating the glossy, wide-open space around them.

"Thank you. I haven't had a chance to come here in a while. But I moved to Barcelona when I was seventeen. Not here. This is new."

"Gorgeous," she said, walking over to one of the large picture windows and looking out at the city below, lit up and in motion.

"Would you like to go out?" he asked.

"What else haven't you done, Rodriguez?"

He crossed from where he was standing and took her hand in his, leaning in and pressing a soft kiss to her lips. "I haven't done that yet today. It's a shame."

She let out a long breath. "It really is a shame. I'm glad you've rectified it."

"Me too."

"What else haven't you done? No zoo. Anything else?"

She was so sincere, so sweet. He could sense a caring behind her question that he wasn't certain he'd ever experienced before. It made him uncomfortable. To have her caring for him. Feeling for him.

He moved near her, touching her face, trying to shift the focus back to the physical. "What about you, Carlotta Santina? What haven't you done?"

Her green eyes glittered in the dim light, nothing shy or restrained in her expression. "There are quite a few things I've never done. I've never just wandered around a city. Never just done something for the pure enjoyment of it. Without a real goal beyond simply living."

"I haven't either. Maybe we could share a first?"

"I like that idea very much."

The night air was warm and heavy, the streets of the city teeming with activity. Nightlife in the city was amazing, and Rodriguez had more than taken advantage of his share of it in the past. But this was different. Innocent in a way, and yet, nothing with Carlotta could truly be innocent. Not when his thoughts drifted to the sex every time he looked at her gorgeous curves.

He'd walked through Las Ramblas during the day, but he'd never lingered on the street at night. He was too busy hitting clubs and picking up women back in his college days to do anything as mundane as visiting an open-air market, or enjoying watching street performers.

Nothing about it seemed mundane tonight. Not with Carlotta, wide-eyed and grinning at his side. They blended in here, not royal, not anything but one of the crowd of hundreds milling around in the wide-open boulevard.

Music from the surrounding restaurants and clubs bled out onto the street, mixing, but not blending, adding to the chaotic atmosphere.

"This is amazing," Carlotta said. "A definite first for me."

"Me too."

She leaned into him, her hand slipping easily into his, her cheek pressed against his shoulder. He leaned down and kissed the top of her head, the action natural, casual in a way he'd never been with a woman before. But he found he liked it. Liked it a lot.

"Oh, Rodriguez, let's go look at the dancer!"

She tugged on his hand and led him through the crowd toward the sound of a guitar rising above the thumping techno music echoing from the clubs.

There was a woman, standing in a clear spot on the cobblestones, a man to her left playing the guitar. She was dancing, high heels stomping hard on the ground, her red dress flaring up to the top of her thighs.

"She's beautiful," Carlotta said, a wistful note in her voice.

"Not more beautiful than you are." It was the truth, and it was usually what a woman wanted to hear when she said something like that.

"No she's…it's different. She's so…free. Everything is so…open and out there. Her passion for life."

"I have tasted your passion, Carlotta." He leaned in and kissed her temple. "You are like living fire in my arms. You don't have to hide anything from me."

She looked at him, her eyes bright. "I can't. You take my control from me."

"It's mutual."

"I'm glad."

"Passion is beautiful," he said, looking at the dancer again. "Your passion is beautiful." He turned his attention back to Carlotta. "It is a shame you were ever made to feel differently."

She smiled at him and he felt it down deep, like a punch in the gut. "I'm learning to see things a bit differently."

Dios. Her smile. He felt strange now. Lighter and heavier at the same time. He wasn't sure how she accomplished things like that. "Do you want dinner?"

"Dinner would be lovely."

He ordered them both beer and tapas and set the baskets on an outdoor table. They were surrounded by street performers dressed as trees, every so often a tree would bend in a different direction. It made everything seem surreal. Not quite of the world he knew. It fit nicely with the things Carlotta was making him feel. "Very good," she said, taking a bite of salted cod.

"What do you think of your first real out-on-the-town experience?"

"Amazing. And what did you think of your first trip to the zoo?"

"I enjoyed it. Even more because of how Luca seemed to get so much out of everything. Especially the lions."

"He's had nightmares about them on and off, don't ask me why, because I'm not really sure. I don't think I ever could have talked him into seeing them in person."

"You think I did?"

"He's different around you. He seems…confident. It's cute."

"I was trying to think what my father might have done if I was afraid of lions," Rodriguez said, not sure why he'd spoken the words out loud. He cleared his throat. "He wouldn't have thrown me in the cage, obviously, since I'm the heir. But… he believed in making me a man."

Carlotta frowned, her well-groomed brows pulled together. "He wouldn't have scared you…."

"Sure he would have. If he thought it would make me into the kind of man who could lead Santa Christobel as he sees fit. As it is, I'm sure he will be disappointed. Well, no, he won't. Because he won't be alive to see it," he said, trying to keep his tone light. Dismissive.

Carlotta studied his face, her heart feeling too large for her chest. After last night she couldn't deny feeling nothing for him. It wasn't just the sex, it was everything. The fact that he'd listened. The fact that she'd even wanted to tell him.

Then today, with Luca. She was right, Luca did scare him, even if she didn't fully understand why. But the way he was with him, the way he tried, that touched her. He might be a natural charmer with women, but he wasn't with children.

Even so, that panic, the way he talked about his father, it all made her feel slightly sick. She didn't really want to ask more. And yet she felt like she had to. Because…she'd told him everything. She wanted to know who he was.

"You seem to know about everything fun in Barcelona. Tell me about it," she said, deciding it was probably a neutral enough topic.

"About what?"

"You. Your penthouse. Why you moved here when you were seventeen."

"Teenagers always want to get away, right?"

"I didn't. I was really good. Until I turned twenty-three. But Natalia was more like that."

"She's your twin?"

"Yes. But we aren't really alike at all. We aren't really very close anymore either. I blamed her for a while but, to be honest, I think I did my share of distancing. I mean, I talk to everyone, but when you're hiding something how close can you really be? I feel like I've been guarding my secret and licking my wounds for the past six years. Hard to maintain meaningful relationships when you're that busy...hiding."

"I imagine. I don't maintain any, so it's never been a problem."

"Oh. So, you didn't make a lot of friends here?"

"I did. I went to college here. Had a lot of friends. Lots of girlfriends. I was able to feel normal for a while. I had a lot of fun here."

"I take it you didn't have fun in Santa Christobel."

He frowned. "I don't feel at home there."

"This place reminds me more of you," she said. Barcelona was alive. Casual and fun. It lacked the pomp and circumstance of his home country.

"I don't feel at home here either," he said. "Don't look at me like that."

"Like what?" She took another bite of her fish.

"Like I'm a wounded puppy. I have never been concerned with concepts of home and family. I have nothing to complain about. I had food. I had shelter. Plenty of people don't have that."

"That's not all people need."

"Sure it is. I came to Barcelona for fun. To get away from my father. Common story," he said. He made it sound light. Casual. He was very good at that. But she knew it wasn't. Because it was there again, that horrible bleakness in his eyes.

He was so good at being charming. At bringing everything back to surface. He had charisma and the power to pretend in a way she could never hope to match. But he was pretending.

She looked down at the basket of food in front of her. "My father expected a lot from me. I don't think either of my parents expected anything from Natalia past a certain point. They just sort of rolled their eyes at her antics. And in some ways, that put more on me. I envied her, a lot. I think it may have been when I really started feeling distant from her. My father especially wanted me to be perfect. Like I was the redemption for the pair of us. When I got pregnant…I'd never seen him like that before. He was so…so angry with me. So disappointed. It hurt more than losing what I'd imagined I had with Gabriel."

"This is the part where I share?" he asked, dark eyebrow lifted.

"I thought you might."

"My father didn't know what to do with a child. He was alone with me. He made mistakes."

"That's all?"

"That's all."

"I don't believe you."

"It's not a big deal, Carlotta," he said, his teeth gritted, his hand drawn into a fist. He unfolded it, flexed his fingers out straight. "He felt that I needed to represent the country. I was his heir. His only child. When my mother left, it became very apparent I would be the only son. That made things more…important."

His tone was even, his expression flat. And the ice in his eyes chilled her through to her bones.

"What did he do to you?" she asked, setting her fork down on the table. "What did he do, Rodriguez?"

He kept his focus on his hand, opening and closing it. "I had to learn to sit still. To be silent, unless I was spoken to."

"Well, you know Luca. How can you possibly…?" She stopped short, the words sticking in her throat. "How?"

He swallowed, his Adam's apple moving, his jaw clenched tight. "It took training." His voice was soft, even, but there was something dark in his tone. "My father had Andalusians. Spirited horses. But he managed to break them. He never hesitated to order that the whip be used." He looked up from his hand, dark eyes locked with hers. "Luckily, he didn't manage to break me. But I did learn when to keep still."

"Rodriguez…he didn't…"

"He didn't use the horsewhip on me, *dios*, no. He had a metal rod that he would slap across my shins when I got too restless. It left bruises, but it didn't damage anything." His words, spoken so casually, as though he were reading from a book. Telling the story of someone else's life. He seemed utterly removed from it. Determined to stay that way.

"He didn't damage anything physically," she said quietly.

"Like I said, Carlotta, we all have our issues. I never went hungry. I never slept out in the cold."

Anger flooded her, filled her, for him, for the child he'd been. For the man he was. "You dismiss it like that, but what if someone were doing that to Luca?"

The glint in Rodriguez's eyes turned to ice. "It would be the last thing he ever did." He stood from the table. "We should go. We will be flying back to Santa Christobel early."

"Oh…I…"

He leaned over and picked up her basket, still full of food. "I have lost my appetite."

Carlotta watched Rodriguez close himself off from her, and she felt her heart splinter in her chest, shards of her soul cracking. He walked ahead of her, and she felt like he was taking some of the broken pieces with him. She felt like she'd found a piece of herself, and lost it all at once.

She walked quickly, closing the gap between them. He looked on ahead, not touching her, not acknowledging her. As though he had shut off a switch inside himself. If only she could do the same. She ached, inside and out, for Rodriguez.

For what he'd been through. And he was pretending it didn't matter.

But it was what he did. She could see that. See it and understand it in a way. Because she'd lived that way to a certain extent. What was the point of bleeding for everyone to see when no one could staunch the flow? So much easier to keep the pain inside. To nurture it, as she did. Or to pretend it wasn't there, like Rodriguez did.

And both of them had been doing it alone for so long, neither of them seemed to know how to bring another person into the mix without upending their perfect order.

That was why he'd walked away. He was trying to hang on to the facade he'd created.

Now she had to decide if she was going to let him.

CHAPTER NINE

BACK at the penthouse, Rodriguez headed straight for his room, closing the door behind him. He needed to think. Needed to process. Needed to figure out why he'd shared all of that with Carlotta. It didn't matter. It didn't.

"Rodriguez?"

He turned at the sound of Carlotta's soft, sweet voice. She was standing in the doorway, one hand clutching the frame as though she were keeping herself from turning and running. No, he couldn't actually imagine that. Carlotta didn't run.

He finished shrugging his shirt off and let it fall to the floor. "What?" She just stared at him, green eyes filled with sadness. Pity. For him? For the boy he'd been? He didn't want that.

"Don't look at me like that," he said, more roughly than he'd intended.

"Like what?"

"Like you want to put a Band-Aid on it and

make it better. I'm not crying over it, Carlotta. Neither should you."

"I'm not crying," she said, her voice breaking on the last word.

He huffed out a laugh. "My father…he was a terrible father. I don't know what I can offer to Luca, but I know I won't be abusive. I understand that what happened to me wasn't right. But I'm not dwelling."

"You don't think it affects you at all?"

He shrugged, even as a slug of pain hit him in the chest. "No. It was all a long time ago. I moved away when I was a teenager, but even before that, my father hadn't raised his hand to me in years."

He ignored how exposed he felt and worked his belt free of the buckle, tugging it off and throwing it down with his shirt. He wasn't going to do a "sharing your feelings and hug" thing, it wasn't in him.

He moved forward, he didn't worry about what had happened in the past. And until Luca had showed up with his mother, he'd hardly given it a thought in years.

"We all carry the past with us," she said quietly. "And what doesn't kill us makes us stronger."

He moved to where she was standing and touched her bare arm, her skin shockingly smooth beneath his hand. "I don't need psychoanalyzing."

"No?"

He shook his head. "I would take a kiss though." He dug deep in himself and searched for that part of him he'd been clinging to for more than ten years. Tried to find the man who flirted, who knew how to keep everything light and superficial.

But Carlotta didn't respond, at least not in the way he was used to. She didn't giggle, or look away coquettishly. She stared at him, her eyes locked with his, serious, intense.

She put her hands on his face, her fingers stroking the back of his neck. When her lips touched his, it wasn't soft, or tentative. She claimed him, her mouth hard on his, her tongue teasing the seam of his lips, demanding entry. A command he couldn't deny.

He met her kiss, met and matched each thrust of her tongue, wrapped his arm around her waist and pulled her into the room, against his body.

He gripped the door with his other hand and closed it firmly before pressing her against it. She arched into him, full, gorgeous breasts pressed tightly against his chest. This wasn't quite the harmless flirtation he'd been looking for.

This was dark. Intense. Something both of them seemed unable to fight. If either of them cared to. At the moment, he certainly didn't.

She moved her hands over his chest, his back, his buttocks, the touch teasing and tormenting him. He rocked against her, right where he knew she wanted him, for her, for him. To ease some of the building, blinding pressure that was threatening to make him come from the pleasure of a simple kiss.

A kiss hadn't excited him so much since he was a teenager. And for some reason, he felt like one now. Felt like he was on the edge of exploding if he didn't have her now. Hot and hard, against the door.

But along with that feeling came the overwhelming need to deny his own pleasure. Something that was even more foreign.

He was a considerate lover, and his partners always left well pleasured, but their satisfaction was never his primary concern. His own was. That was why he engaged in casual affairs. Because they each took responsibility for themselves, for their needs, the things that turned them on, they pursued their own pleasures, using the other person as an aid to that.

He did it. The women he slept with did the same.

But it wasn't what he wanted now. He wanted to give her pleasure. He wanted to watch her face. He could remember how she'd looked last night when they were together, how she looked when she was completely lost in pleasure.

Just the thought made his erection pulse.

He gritted his teeth and pulled away from her, his body protesting. "It'll be over too fast if we keep going like this."

"I'm fine with fast," she said, her hands on his chest. "I never have been before. It's never been like this. With you...all it takes is a look and I'm so close."

"Me too," he said. Not something he'd normally admit. But it was pointless to deny it when his entire body was trembling with need that was poised on the brink of becoming satisfaction. But it wouldn't be true satisfaction. Not the kind he needed, not the kind he craved. The kind that would only come from bringing her with him.

She pushed the strap of her summer dress down, pulling one arm through, then the other, so the dress was simply hanging from her curves. So easy to tug it down, to reveal her amazing body to his gaze.

He clenched his hands into fists and kept them glued to his sides. Determined to watch. To let her control the pace. For now.

She let the dress fall, her curves covered only by a whisper-thin, lacy bra and panty set. The kind that seemed designed to frame and accentuate a woman's body, rather than conceal anything.

"I didn't think…after what happened tonight…I didn't think you'd want this. Want me," she said.

"Oh, I want you," he said, swallowing hard. He extended his hand, tensed his muscles to try and disguise the trembling there, and touched the lace edge of her bra, trailing his finger along the line where fine fabric met silken flesh. "Make no mistake, I want you."

That same sort of heaviness hung in the air, the same kind he'd felt last night. But rather than turning from it, he let it drive him. Feeding the hunger that was growing inside of him until it was a yawning chasm of need that he wasn't certain he could ever satisfy.

He lowered his head, tracing the path his finger had just followed with the tip of his tongue. Carlotta shuddered beneath his touch and he felt her deep, intense response resonate within him. Her pleasure becoming his own. Her desire filling him, making his body tight and hard with lust.

"Your body is so amazing. So perfect."

She laughed, a tight, strained sound. "It doesn't look like it used to. Childbirth does that to you."

He lowered himself onto his knees and pressed a kiss to her stomach. It wasn't perfectly tight and flat, it was soft, slightly rounded. So feminine and sexy. "Like I said, it is perfection."

She put her hand on his bicep, fingers moving over the ridges of muscle. "You aren't so bad yourself." She laughed. "Understatement. In fact, I think I'd like to see some more." She put her finger beneath his chin and pushed up. He stood, the pressure not enough to force his movements in any way, but he responded as though it did. "Take off your clothes," she said, her eyes locked on his.

"Are you always like this?"

She shook her head. "Never. But you make me feel different."

She made him feel different too. But he was damned if he'd admit. Not when he could hardly understand it, or even put words to it.

"I like it," he said. Instead of the other things he could have said. Because he did like it. And it was the simplest truth he had.

"Good."

He shrugged his pants and underwear down and stood in front of her. He'd never thought that much about being naked in front of a woman, but he'd felt exposed since their conversation at dinner. And now, he felt like she was looking inside him. As if she could truly see him.

She moved to him, her fingers sliding over his abs and down to his rock-hard erection. He put his hand over hers, halting her movements. "Carlotta, I'm too close," he gritted.

"I'm okay with that," she said, squeezing him.

She leaned in and kissed his neck, her tongue hot and slick against his skin. Everything felt heightened, his blood running hot and fast just beneath the surface of his skin.

"I'm not. I need…"

She continued down, her hand caressing him, her lips and tongue on his chest, his stomach. Then she braced her hands on his thighs, holding him tight as she flicked the tip of her tongue against the head of his arousal.

He sifted his fingers through her hair with the intent of pulling her back, but he couldn't. He could only hold on to her, keep his knees from buckling as she took the length of him into her mouth.

His muscles shook beneath her sensual assault, her hand working in time with her mouth. Fire built in him, low and liquid, spreading through him, bringing him to the brink. Then she would pause, squeeze him hard, and it would ebb, keep it at bay. Somehow she knew just when to pause, knew how to give him just enough to time. Knew how to bring him to the edge without letting him go over.

It was torture. Beautiful, decadent torture. And he couldn't remember ever being so turned on in his life.

Carlotta moaned, deep and low, the sound moving through his body, adding to the sensation. He tightened his grip on her hair and earned another throaty sound from Carlotta.

"Enough," he said tightly.

She raised her head, a satisfied smile curving her lips. She stood, wrapping her arms around his neck, looking him in the eye. He took the chance to unhook her bra and slide her panties down her legs, reveling in the feeling of soft, bare skin against his.

She moved to the bed, stretching out before him across the dark comforter, her smile wicked. A temptation. His pulse was pounding, in time with her name, repeating over and over in his mind. Carlotta. He was so very aware that it was her he wanted, not simply sex and satisfaction, but Carlotta.

His stomach rebelled at the thought. She couldn't be allowed to be that important. He couldn't think straight, and his chest felt full. All of the emotions he'd been battling since she walked into his life felt too close to the surface. Too raw. This was everything he feared, everything he'd spent his life learning to deny.

He looked at her face, her beautiful face. He felt as though someone had reached inside him and twisted his guts. He had to stop it. Had to build the wall back up.

"Turn over," he said, his voice rough.

For one moment her confidence faltered.

"Trust me, Carlotta."

"I do," she said.

Her admission made him feel like a knife had just been pushed into his chest. He ignored it, tried to breathe around the sharp, searing pain. Tried to embrace the deep, dark nothing he knew still lived in him.

She turned over onto her stomach, and for a moment, he felt like he could breathe again. The emotional knot in his chest loosened. He needed to distance himself, but at the same time, he needed to be inside her more than he needed air.

He joined her on the bed, his legs on either side of hers. He traced the line of her back with his fingertips, pressed a kiss to her shoulder blade, while his hand skimmed over her curves, palming her soft buttocks.

She moaned and he moved his hand around so that he was touching her stomach, then lower still so that he could caress the bundle of nerves at the apex of her thighs. "Up on your knees," he said.

She complied, her bottom coming into contact with the hard ridge of his arousal. He bit back a curse as he continued to stroke her, pushing one finger into her slick folds as he reached over to the side table with his other, pulling a condom out of the drawer.

"Ready?" he asked.

"Yes." She breathed the word.

He brought the head of his shaft against the slick entrance to her body and entered her slowly, not wanting to cause her any discomfort, not even for a moment.

"Yes," she said, a sound of satisfaction this time, and he began to thrust in and out of her body.

He held her hip with one hand, while the other was moving over her in time with his strokes. He could hear nothing, think of nothing, beyond the amazing, white-hot blaze of pleasure that was coursing through his body.

"Rodriguez." Every syllable of his name was filled with the evidence of her satisfaction as her internal muscles pulsed around him.

And then he was pushed back into reality, no cocoon of denial to shield him. This was Carlotta.

And it was more than sexual pleasure coursing through his veins.

"Carlotta." He gave in to the blinding urge to say her name, to acknowledge the depth of the desire that seemed to be driving him. And when he did that, he gave his body permission to release, his orgasm overtaking him, tearing away every last shred of control that he'd wrapped himself in.

He clung to her as he rode the wave, froze as he emptied himself, his muscles shaking in the aftermath, his heart pounding so hard he was certain she could hear it. He took a few steadying breaths.

"I'll be right back," he said, glad for the need to go and dispose of the condom. Glad for the excuse to gain some distance.

But even when he closed the door to the bathroom he could still feel her. On his skin. Beneath it. He felt tangled in her.

Sex had never done this to him. He'd always held himself back from it, engaging his body but never anything more.

Tonight, he had nearly drowned in the experience. The emotion overtaking the physical, fusing with it, creating a force he could not deny or control.

He had always prided himself on being a man in control, from the time he'd been a boy and control meant the difference between flying under the radar and enduring a beating.

And Carlotta had stripped him of it. Effortlessly, it seemed. And he had not been able to rebuild it. He had been left defenseless. Open and bleeding, raw. Exposed. Vulnerable.

He had vowed he would never be vulnerable again. That no one would ever hold power over him. Have the power to cause him pain.

He discarded the condom and turned on the shower, stepping beneath the cold spray, not waiting for it to heat.

He couldn't lose his control. He could not allow it. He hit his fist against the tile wall, welcoming the bite of pain. Anything to bring him back down, to erase the buzz of arousal that was still coursing through him.

Anything to remind him of who he was, and all that he could never hope to have.

CHAPTER TEN

I'm going to have a busy week when we get back home. Rodriguez had said it, and he'd meant it.

After they returned to Santa Christobel, Rodriguez became the man he'd promised to be from the beginning. A man leading a separate life from her.

In the past week he hadn't even come to her at night.

And no matter how much she'd hoped to stay detached, she just wasn't.

Maybe if Carlotta had any clue what she wanted she'd be able to talk to Rodriguez and get everything sorted out. But it all came back down to the fact that she wasn't supposed to care that he was being kept busy with affairs of state.

She blew out a breath and took her cell phone out of her purse, toying with the idea of calling Sophia. It had been too long since she'd talked to her sister. Mostly because it was so much easier to send a text and feign happiness.

And then there was Natalia. Natalia who, at this point, was more like a stranger than a twin these days.

Now she felt even more alone. Great, nice train of thought.

She had Luca, she was comfortable. She was home with him. She shouldn't care that her sisters were in different countries and Rodriguez was barely speaking to her. Of course, she did care. But she didn't know what to do about that.

She scrolled through a litany of her favorite swear words, in English and Italian, while she watched Luca hopping over a ball in the middle of the expansive lawn from her position on the terrace.

"Watch me!" he shouted as he launched himself over the bright red rubber ball.

"Be careful, Luca," she said. It was almost reflexive to say that, whenever he said, "Watch me."

"I am!"

"Yeah, okay," she said, rolling her eyes, thankful he couldn't see her perform the childish action. She was supposed to be the mom. But she wasn't perfect, even though she tried to be.

She thought of Natalia again, of all the confusing emotion wrapped up in that relationship. Another area of her life she'd been imperfect in. She'd so envied the bright light her sister possessed that she managed to just laugh off the stuff the tabloids wrote about her. That she seemed to have permission, even if it was grudging, to be who she wanted to be. To be who she was instead of trying to force herself into a mold she would never, ever fit into.

But that wasn't Natalia's fault. Carlotta realized that for the first time. Natalia wasn't doing it to her, to hurt her in any way. She was simply living. And Carlotta's own issues were a big part of what kept them so distant from each other.

She scrolled through the numbers on her phone, her fingers trembling. Maybe she should call her. Maybe it was time.

Her phone vibrated in her hand. She looked down and saw Natalia's name on the screen and her heart banged against her chest. It made sense now, why Natalia's name had been so persistent in her mind. She was thinking of her too. But if her sister was calling, the news had to be bad. Something catastrophic, because Natalia never called.

She answered quickly. "Natalia?"

"*Ciao*, Lotta."

No one had called her Lotta in years. No one had been close enough to her to use a nickname. It made her throat feel tight, achy.

"Natalia, what's wrong?"

"Nothing," her sister said, far too quickly. "Congratulations on your engagement."

Carlotta looked down at the ring on her left hand. Oh, yes, she was engaged. But if not for the memory of those two glorious nights in Rodriguez's bed she wouldn't believe it.

But Natalia hadn't called to congratulate her, and her sister's skirting of the issue was getting on her already frayed nerves. She closed her eyes and worked to cultivate a calm tone. "Natalia. Something is wrong, I can tell by your voice. What is it?"

Even after years of distance, Natalia's tone was easy to read. They were twins, and regardless of the fact that they were as opposite as two people could be, she had always felt deeply the things

Natalia had felt. Had always sensed when something wasn't right. That also accounted for the restlessness she'd felt a few moments earlier.

"I…" Natalia hesitated. "I just wanted to talk to you. And see how you were doing."

Carlotta didn't believe that for a moment. Her sister was many things, a lot of them good, but after going so long without contact from her, she couldn't really believe she'd suddenly decided she cared about what was happening with her.

I'm falling for the wrong guy again. And I know better. He's probably screwing actresses and models even as we speak, maybe even at the same time, and I'm sitting here feeling like I'm missing half of myself.

"I'm fine," she said, because the truth wasn't going to cut it here. Not when she hated the truth so much.

"Are you really? I mean…this marriage…"

"I'm only doing what we all must do," Carlotta said, her words not her own. They were her father's words. And right now, she hated them. "I'm more worried about you, Natalia, we haven't spoken—"

"In years, I know," her twin said, her tone defensive.

"Not years." But close.

"We haven't had a real conversation in years."

That insight, coming from Natalia, shocked Carlotta a bit. She was right. They hadn't. She hadn't really had a meaningful conversation with anyone but Rodriguez since she'd gotten pregnant with Luca. She'd just sort of closed off. Her sister had noticed. And it had hurt her, she could hear that in her voice.

That cut deep. That her own issues had affected Natalia that way. That she had let her resentments come between them.

"I just wanted to say," Natalia said, her voice unsteady, "I'm sorry for not being there when you had Luca. And after I..." She paused and Carlotta waited, wondering if she should speak, wondering if she could. "I was afraid."

"I know you were, Natalia," Carlotta said, keeping her voice neutral.

"And angry," Natalia continued. "About a lot of things. About how you were treated and how it would change things. I felt like you were moving on to a whole new life without me."

For some reason, Carlotta laughed, even though she felt no humor. Only a bone-deep sadness. "I was, I suppose."

"But I was selfish. I know that."

Carlotta let the words wash over her, felt them loosen the hold on some of the anger that was wrapped around her heart. Anger she hadn't realized was still so prominent, because it had become such a part of her.

"It was a long time ago," she said, more to herself than to Natalia.

"Still, I just…wanted to be honest."

Carlotta swallowed hard, trying to grasp what her sister had said. Trying to make it matter. Trying to let go of the hurt and anger, and hold on to it at the same time.

Not possible, Carlotta. Let it go, or hang on. There's no halfway.

Coming from Natalia, this was big. Huge. And if there was one thing Carlotta knew, it was that everyone deserved forgiveness. Because everyone would need it at some point in time. She had. She'd made mistakes. She hadn't been perfect, and while it had been easy to blame her twin for the erosion of their relationship, the truth was, Carlotta had shut down.

"What's going on, to provoke all this honesty?" she asked finally.

"Nothing," Natalia said. Too quickly. "I've met someone," she amended. "Someone who's challenged me. Someone who's changed me."

That sounded familiar. More than. Enough to make her feel an uncomfortable stab of emotion in her heart. She'd met someone too. And she felt changed. In every way a different woman than the one who'd first arrived in Santa Christobel.

Because of Rodriguez.

"Changed? Are you engaged as well, Natalia?"

"No," she said.

"Natalia," Carlotta tried again, hoping to extract more from her. "Who is this person?" Man, woman, rent boy? But she didn't want to press, or be flippant. This was important. Somehow, this conversation was essential. And it wasn't the subject matter, so much as the fact that they were having one at all.

"Just someone," she said, her tone so sad that Carlotta felt an echo of the pain in her own heart. "No one important."

"Oh."

She hung up with her sister, feeling…everything. Pain for whatever Natalia was going through, but overwhelming happiness too, because of the moment of connection. Also, fear. A lot of fear.

Because she was afraid she and Natalia were going through something far too similar at the moment. She was afraid her feelings for Rodriguez were crossing into the kind of territory she needed to stay out of.

She'd been there, done that, made the papers. Falling in love with the wrong man, making an idiot of herself for him. She didn't intend to do it with her own husband.

What if he really was out sleeping with other women? He'd promised fidelity, but what did that really mean? At least she knew that if Rodriguez promised something, he would mean it. At the time. She also knew a man like him was bound to be a little bit fickle.

He'd said it himself. Sex was cheap.

To him it was. But it was costing her. Bits and pieces of her heart and soul. It probably wasn't even the sex. She hadn't been with him since the night they'd spent together in Barcelona.

It felt like it had been longer. And less time too. She still ached for his touch, and she still felt branded by it. He did the strangest things to her.

"I jumped it!" Luca shouted.

"Yay, Luca!" she returned.

"Good job, Luca."

She whirled around and saw Rodriguez standing in the doorway, and her heart immediately jumped into her throat. He was gorgeous, even when she was kind of mad at him. Even when she was confused about her feelings. She was not confused about the gorgeousness.

He ran his hand over his thick, dark hair, his smile wide and thoroughly sexy. Thoroughly angering too.

"Thanks," Luca said, running up to the terrace, Rodriguez drawing him like a moth to the flame. "Did you have a good day?" Luca asked, his manners on show for once.

Rodriguez's smile turned tight. "I did. You?"

"I jumped over that ball."

"A success then," he said.

"I'm surprised to see you here before dark," Carlotta said, knowing she sounded a little shrewish, and not really caring.

"We have a thing tonight."

"We?" she asked, her voice tight.

"Yes. We. I do not intend to take another woman as my date."

"Some notice would be nice," she practically hissed. "This is becoming a habit with you. I need time to get ready." Oh, she sounded like a nagging wife already and the wedding wasn't taking place for months.

"Three hours should be sufficient."

"I think Angelina had planned on taking the afternoon off. She went out."

"I talked to Angelina."

Annoyance coursed through her. "You talked to Angelina...and you didn't talk to me?"

"Is Angelina going to bring movies?" Luca asked.

"I don't know, Luca," Carlotta said. "What is this thing we're going to?"

"A charity event in the city."

"Can I go?" Luca asked.

Rodriguez looked down at Luca. "You wouldn't like it. You'd have to wear a tie, and you couldn't jump over anything."

Luca made a face. "Then I don't want to go."

"Neither do I," Rodriguez said.

"And we're going because…?" Carlotta asked.

"Because it's a good cause. And apparently my father goes every year. I didn't find out until this afternoon and I came straight home."

"Oh," she said, feeling a bit subdued by that piece of information. "How is your father?" she asked.

"Not well. But not any worse."

"Well…good…I guess."

He shrugged, his emotions as unreadable as ever.

"Rodriguez, will you watch a movie with me?" Luca asked, his green eyes round and earnest.

Rodriguez hesitated for a moment. "Sure, Luca. We can watch something while your mama gets ready."

Luca smiled and grabbed Rodriguez's hand. And then Carlotta really couldn't feel angry at him, because even though he was still tense with Luca, he was trying. That meant everything to her. If he hadn't been able to treat Luca well… there was no way she could have stayed. No way she could agree to marry him.

"I'll see you in a bit," she said, watching as Luca led Rodriguez inside.

And she fell a little harder for him right then.

Rodriguez didn't know when he'd relaxed, but he had. Gradually his muscles had stopped feeling tense. He'd stopped worrying so much about doing the wrong thing.

And then, at some point, Luca had fallen asleep, his head resting against Rodriguez's shoulder. Now, Rodriguez's arm was asleep and Luca's warmth had crossed over into too hot. But he didn't want to move, for fear of waking the little boy.

He also didn't want to analyze exactly what Luca's trust of him made him feel. Or how badly it would hurt when he lost it.

Because he would.

It was part of his life. No one ever maintained a connection with him. At some point he'd just accepted it was something in him, and he'd made it work for him.

But the thought of losing Luca's trust…

At least he wouldn't lose Carlotta's. He seriously doubted he'd ever had it.

"How was the movie?"

He turned his head and saw Carlotta, her dark hair pulled back, large gold earrings highlighting her perfectly made-up features. She was wearing an ethereal white dress with a bold, black geometric pattern on the bodice, so at odds with the sheer, delicate fabric. But the pattern drew the eye to her figure, to her perfect, heavenly curves.

"He slept through most of it," Rodriguez said, forcing the words through his suddenly dry throat.

"I hope he sleeps through the night. It's too late for a nap." She smiled, the look on her face so sweet, so full of love. A look reserved for her son.

He envied it right then. So much that it was physical. Not just because he wished she would look at him with such emotion, but because he wished someone in his life could have. His mother, his father. Someone, anyone.

Holding Luca against him, it was hard to imagine how anyone could strike a child. How someone could abandon a child. He hadn't even been able to move Luca to allow the blood flow to return to his arm, much less leave him in the room by himself. The thought of walking out of his life forever, and leaving him with someone who would treat him horribly…

Not even he could do that, and he'd always considered himself emotionally broken.

"Angelina is here. She's ready to take him."

"Can I carry him to his room?" he asked, a question he hadn't known he was going to ask until he had.

This time, she did smile at him. "Of course."

He scooped Luca up and stood from the couch, crossing the intimate living area, a room that had been designed for family movie viewings and games nights. One that had gone unused by his family.

It was a short walk to Luca's room, and the little boy didn't even stir when Rodriguez laid him in bed and tucked the covers around his still form.

Carlotta leaned in and kissed Luca's forehead before they left the room.

"Sorry about earlier," she said.

"Sorry I wasn't able to tell you sooner." *Sorry I've been gone all week. Sorry I've been unable to face you.*

He didn't say the last part out loud.

"I understand. Things happen. I was…on edge

already." They walked down the stairs and greeted Angelina, who was on her way up, then headed out of the palace. Rodriguez's convertible was parked in front, idling, ready for them. He opened Carlotta's door for her, the subtle hint of perfume and a scent that was uniquely her assaulted him, causing a surge of lust to hit him in the gut.

"Why were you on edge?" he said, as he started the car and maneuvered the vehicle out of the courtyard and through the first gate.

"I talked to Natalia."

"Your twin?"

"Yes. It was…good. I think…" She cleared her throat. "I think we might be on the way to fixing things. And even though she denied it, I think she's met someone special. Natalia needs someone special. I'm happy for her."

"You sound thrilled."

She looked at him, her expression baleful. "It's a lot for one afternoon."

"And Luca jumped over the red ball."

That got a laugh from her. "Yes, he did. Thank goodness for Luca. He makes everything so much… He brings perspective."

"Yes," Rodriguez said. "He does."

"You seemed more comfortable with him tonight."

Carlotta looked at Rodriguez, trying to gauge his reaction. It was impossible, as always. "I'm figuring this all out. I'm not sure what, or who, I'm supposed to be to him yet. Not sure what he'll want from me."

Carlotta had given it a lot of thought too. "I… He'll always have a lot of friends, Rodriguez. And I have brothers, so he'll have uncles. The one thing he'll never have is a father." She swallowed. "Unless you're willing to step into that role."

Rodriguez tightened his hold on the steering wheel, his knuckles turning white as he turned it sharply, driving expertly along the winding country road that bordered the beach.

"I thought…I thought I would be able to keep distant, but he doesn't allow that, does he?"

"No."

"No child will," he said, almost heavily.

"Is that a problem?"

"I was under the impression a wife and children wouldn't alter my life. It didn't seem to alter my father's all that much."

Carlotta looked at her hands. "You're not the

same man as your father, Rodriguez. You must realize that."

"I do," he said, his voice rusty.

"Then it shouldn't surprise you that you can't ignore us quite as easily as your father was able to ignore you and your mother."

"He ignored me until my mother left. Then I became…a target of some kind. The way you look at Luca…I've never understood how she could leave me with him. And now, seeing you with him… she did not love me like that."

"Not every person is meant to be a parent."

"No," he said. "I suppose that's true."

"I'm sorry," she said. And she was, truly, deeply, the pain of his childhood running through her bones, making her ache for him. "You should have been given better. And I know you say it doesn't matter. But it does. They owed you more than they gave you."

"Perhaps. Perhaps not."

She didn't understand the cryptic statement and she didn't have time to ask before he turned the radio on, effectively ending the conversation.

She wished he wouldn't close down on her. She wanted him, all of him. She'd given herself to him, not just her body, but her secrets. Everything in her.

He had her heart. She didn't want to admit it. Not to herself, and definitely not to him, but there wasn't much point in denying it. She was in love with Rodriguez. Not the man he pretended to be, the man he showed the world, but the man he was inside.

The man she sensed beneath that light, flirtatious facade. The man who had listened to her darkest secrets without even a hint of judgment. The man who had made love to her with such passion and fire she thought it would consume her.

The man who took her son to the zoo. Who held him while he slept.

The man he didn't want her to see. The man he didn't seem to want to be.

They drove on in silence, and Carlotta kept her eyes glued to the lights of the city, drawing closer as they drove down the beach highway.

The charity event was being held in Santa Christobel's famous gardens. An expansive, outdoor area with flowers and plants from most of the world's tropical locales.

Rodriguez pulled the car up to the front of the

walled garden, and gave his keys to the valet. He came around to her side, ever the charming gentleman, and helped her from the vehicle. She shivered when his hand touched her bare arm. He hadn't touched her in a week. She missed his touch.

Missed his kiss. Missed him most of all.

She ignored the vast well of longing that opened up in her and followed him into the event. The air inside the walls of the garden was thick and perfumed. The expansive lawn area lit up by white paper lanterns.

People were standing around, laughing, talking. Drinking. It was a light event, and money was flowing out of wealthy pockets and into the charity, which was nice to see.

Except she wasn't able to feel as happy about it as she should. Because she was still turning over their conversation in her mind. Trying to dissect it, to find the meaning.

They owed you more than they gave you.
Perhaps not.

Did he really think he hadn't deserved more than a mother who abandoned him and a father who beat him? How was that even possible?

Rodriguez, at their first meeting at least, had seemed arrogant. Full of himself. The kind of man who thought women falling at his feet, or into his bed, was his due. Not the kind of man who would think he deserved the treatment his parents had shown him.

Yet in those moments when she'd glimpsed the haunting emptiness in his eyes, she'd known there was more to him than that. More than that thin facade he wrapped around himself like a cloak.

"Drink?" he asked, pulling two glasses of champagne from a passing waiter's tray without waiting for her answer.

She took it from him. "I thought we agreed that the refreshments at things like this were…"

"Awful?"

"That."

"Alcohol is still alcohol. It makes everything more fun, right?" he asked, his tone clipped.

"I don't know if that's a healthy attitude," she said, sensing a recklessness in him that shocked her. Bothered her a bit.

"Maybe not. But then, I'm not really renowned for healthy attitudes, am I?"

Whatever was on his mind was prevented from

escaping by the people who came to talk to them. Everyone wanted a piece of the Crown Prince. The man who would soon be their king. And, of course, she was a fascination as well, since she was wearing his ring.

Carlotta could sense Rodriguez's growing annoyance and she tried to maintain her civility, tried to be friendly to the guests since he didn't seem to be in the mood to play nice.

"What's wrong with you?" she hissed when one well-wisher departed.

"I'm not in the mood for all of this." He turned his dark gaze to her. "I want to be alone with you."

"You've had all week to be alone with me. You avoided me."

He trailed his finger along the line of her jaw. "A mistake, I think."

"Do you?" she asked, her voice flat.

"Carlotta." He leaned in and his cell phone rang. "*Un momento. Hola….Sì….*How long does he have?...Why did no one tell me?" He paused for a moment. "We'll be there in a moment." He snapped the phone shut, his gaze not meeting hers. "We have to go. It's my father. He's…We have to go."

CHAPTER ELEVEN

THE king was in a private wing of the hospital, but it was still very much a hospital. White, pastel and sterile. Carlotta hadn't been in many hospitals.

She hadn't been back to one since Luca was born. She was thankful for it.

The environment was unsettling, the smell of antiseptic stinging her nose. Even more unsettling was the dark emotion rolling off Rodriguez.

When they arrived at his father's room, the priest was there, standing by to administer last rites. Carlotta's stomach clenched tight. This was very likely it, and she knew that Rodriguez wasn't ready. How could he be ready?

Her own father was a tyrant in many ways, and yet, she still couldn't fathom the thought of losing him.

"I will go in alone," he said, his voice hard.

Carlotta stayed outside the room, leaning against the wall, her hands clasped tightly in front of her,

her heart pounding hard in her chest, tears threatening to fall. Her throat burned with the effort of keeping them back.

She watched the hands on the clock turn. Watched the priest go in, and come back out. Felt her heart sinking lower.

She finally moved to a chair, felt her eyes growing heavy.

"It's done, Carlotta." Rodriguez's thick voice shook her from the sleep she hadn't realized she'd fallen into.

"What? No," she said, her heart aching.

"He's gone." Rodriguez's face was set, his expression immovable, flat as though it had been carved from stone.

"Rodriguez, I'm…"

"Let's go," he said.

She stood from the chair, trying to shake off the dizziness that came from being jerked out of such a deep sleep.

She followed him out of the hospital and into the cold night air. She felt her body start to shake. "I don't… What do we do now? What does this mean?"

"We'll hold a press conference. First thing in the morning. And I am king." He walked to where he had parked his car, at the front of the hospital. He had not used a parking space, and no one had corrected him.

He jerked the driver's side door open, then froze. "And my father is gone."

She rounded the car and threw her arms around him, not caring if it was what he wanted or not. He needed it, even if he would never admit it.

"I'm sorry," she whispered, her voice breaking.

One of his arms came around her, his hand resting on her back. She felt his sharp intake of breath against her chest.

"I'm sorry," she said again, holding him to her. Just holding him.

The chill night wind blew in from the sea, cold and wet, salty. It blended with the tears on her cheeks. She squeezed his hand. "Do you want to walk for a while?"

"Yes," he said.

He kept hold of her hand, and they left the car, the door standing open. Everything seemed deserted this late. The hospital was out of the city by a couple of minutes, nestled in the hills, by the ocean. She and Rodriguez walked through the lot, to where it ended and a path began, through the grass and down to the sand. Neither of them spoke until they were standing at the edge of the ocean, the waves lapping near their feet.

"My father is gone," he said again. "And there is no chance of…fixing what passed between us. No chance at reconciliation. No chance for him to…apologize. He never would have, but the possibility was there. And it's gone now. That was all I will ever have with my father. A childhood filled with pain and fear, and then years of stony silence when I avoided him as much as I possibly could."

He sucked in a sharp breath. "I do not know what to feel. If I should feel anything at all."

"There's no right or wrong answer," she said. "Just…whatever you feel. That's what you're supposed to feel."

He didn't speak. He lowered himself to the sand and sat. Carlotta sat with him, not caring that she was getting sand on her dress. Not caring about anything but being next to him. Comforting him.

Rodriguez tried to breathe past the tightness in his chest. He wasn't certain he could. Everything with his father was final now, and with that re-alization came both relief and a grief that went down into his bones. Made them hurt.

"I have…simplified things," he said slowly, not sure why he was sharing with her, but certain he could no longer hold it in. "I have dealt with my father on my terms, when I could. Separating my-self from who I was, who he was, when I was a child. But it was never simple. I thought I could bury it. Make it so that it didn't matter so I could deal with him at functions, in interviews. But so much of me hated him, Carlotta. For what he did to me. For making my mother leave."

His voice broke and he felt weak, humiliat-ing emotion overpowering him, felt moisture in his eyes he couldn't blame on the ocean spray. "Because she couldn't live with a monster and I know, I understand, that she never could have taken his heir from him. But it was easier to be mad at her because she was gone. I didn't have to try to exist with her."

Carlotta put her hand on the back of his neck, her touch strengthening him.

"When she left…he took my toys. Because I was bad, he said. My mother left because I was bad, and a bad boy didn't deserve toys." He'd never told anyone any of this. He'd made himself believe it was stupid. Unimportant. At least he'd tried to force himself to believe it. "And after that, a while after, he hit me for the first time. For fidgeting in church. We're supposed to set an example, you see, and I wasn't being an example. I was Luca's age then. Barely five. That's why I learned to shut it all down. And I never have figured out how to feel…normal again."

She leaned her head against him, her face in the crook of his neck. He felt the dampness of her tears on his skin.

"I'm supposed to be sad," he said. "That he's gone. But all I'm really sad about is that he'll never be my father. Not really. It's finished now. My mother…for all I know she's gone too. I can't ever have it back, and I think part of me believed that I would."

She put her arms around him then and he realized he'd never shared his sadness with anyone before. Had never been held while he cried, or while he felt like crying. Not for as long as he could remember.

He'd never had anyone to listen to him.

He'd invited countless women into his bed, but not into him. He'd never shown anyone who he was. And now she knew. She knew how broken he was. That his own mother had left him, that his father had beaten him.

That his parents had never loved him. His own parents.

A violent pain stabbed at his heart. His own parents hadn't loved him. What must be wrong with him? No wonder he'd ignored feeling for so many years. Damn his father for making him feel again. And Carlotta too.

He pulled away from her, standing, his breath coming hard and fast, his entire body heavy, on fire, as though it were filled with hot lead. Burning him. Weighing him down.

"Rodriguez…"

"No," he said sharply. "You can't make this better. We're not going to have a…a phone call reconciliation like you were able to do with your sister. It's not fixable. It's done."

He turned and walked off the beach. Cursing and kicking his shoes off when they filled with sand, walking the rest of the way to the car in his bare feet, the rocks biting into his flesh, his shoes abandoned.

He got into the car and slammed the door. He waited until Carlotta slid in beside him. He started the engine and pulled out of the hospital lot, his entire body tight, on the verge of breaking.

Neither of them spoke on the ride back to the palace. He wished she would. He wanted to draw strength from her and he hated himself for it. Hated the dependence.

Hated that, somehow, he'd let his emotions start functioning again. And they were eating him alive now.

He didn't care that when he pulled into the palace courtyard he sprayed gravel on the lawn by turning too sharply. He didn't care that the servants stared at him, openmouthed, when he walked through the halls, without shoes.

He went into his room and closed the door firmly behind him. Never looking back. Hardly seeing anything.

He wanted Carlotta. For all he knew she was still sitting down in the car. He wanted her with a ferocity that denied everything he believed about himself.

But tonight, everything he'd tried to make himself was coming unraveled.

No, not just tonight. From the first moment he'd seen Carlotta. Everything, the carefully laid plans, the vague concept of a wife he hardly noticed, one who didn't interfere…it had all started to erode. And right now, he needed her so badly he couldn't regret it.

He tore open the door to his room and stalked down the hall, taking his shirt off and letting it fall to the marble floor as he did. He pushed open the door to Carlotta's room without knocking.

She whirled around, her eyes wide. She was wearing a cotton nightgown. One she'd probably just put on. He wanted it off.

"I need you," he said, the admission torn from him.

She nodded slowly and moved across the room and into his arms, kissing him with just the right amount of pressure. Somehow she knew what he needed. She always knew.

Her fingers skated over the skin on his back, teasing him, tantalizing him, getting him hot. Pushing away the conflicting knot of emotions with a fire of need that started to burn in his gut and spread through him, cleansing him. Making things seem clearer. Simpler.

She kissed his neck, his collarbone, hands moving to his bare chest, skimming his nipples.

He looked down at her lovely face, stoic with concentration. The burning in his stomach intensified.

"Do you want me?" he asked.

"Yes," she said, her eyes meeting his.

"Not, do you want to fix me? Do you want me?"

"Of course I do."

He held her away from his body, the desperation in him real, overtaking everything else. "I don't want pity sex, dammit. I want you. I want you to want *me*. Like I want you. Not because you're supposed to be my wife, or because you feel sorry me."

"From the moment I met you, I wanted you. You steal my control, Rodriguez. Wholly and completely," she said, her voice steady. "And I want you now, just like I have every time. Not because anyone's forcing me. As much as you need me right now, I need you just as much. If you told me I could walk away from this, from us, our marriage, right now, I wouldn't. I'm in this with you.

For life. I promised it, and I will keep that promise," she vowed.

"Make me forget." He buried his face in her hair, breathing in heavily.

"Don't forget who you're with."

"I want your face to be the only thing I can remember. Your touch. Your face. You, Carlotta, nothing else," he said, lowering his head, pressing a kiss to her cleavage. "Please."

She stepped back and tugged the nightgown over her head, consigning it to the floor while he did the same with the rest of his clothes.

He got into bed with her, sliding beneath the covers, the sheets soft on his skin, her bare body even softer.

He ran his hands over her curves, inhaled her scent, so unique, so Carlotta. "I want you, Carlotta Santina," he said. "Only you."

"I want you, Rodriguez Anguiano." She pressed a kiss to his lips, her tongue sliding along the seam of his mouth.

He put his hand beneath her bottom and she parted her thighs, granting him access. He slid into her hot, wet body, pleasure, emotion, crashing over him. He shuddered as she enveloped him, her arms, her legs, trapping him against her.

They moved in rhythm, their breath blending, hearts pounding in time. She met each of his thrusts, her hands linked with his, fingers laced together.

They reached the peak together, their sounds of pleasure mingling in the quiet room.

And then he held her to him, his breathing fractured, harsh. His heart pounding, the fire in him burning even hotter now than before, edging everything out. Everything but the need for Carlotta, not for sex, that desire was satisfied for now. But for her. To be in her arms. In her bed. Just with her.

Her legs tangled with his, her heavy, satisfied sigh bringing him even more pleasure than his climax had.

For now, at least, things seemed good.

And hopefully, by morning, he could have his walls rebuilt. Could turn off the emotion, the need, the deep, heavy desire for more than a man like him could ever hope to have.

CHAPTER TWELVE

"I'M SORRY."

Carlotta opened her eyes and looked up into Rodriguez's handsome, tormented face. Everything from the night before came flooding back.

"Why?" she asked, rolling to her side, not caring that the sheets had fallen to her waist.

"I was…not myself last night."

"You were in pain," she said. "Your father…"

"It's still no excuse for how I spoke to you."

"Rodriguez, I'm not mad at you for that. I… We hadn't slept together in a week. I get that the timing looked a little bit suspect. But I did want you. I do. I don't regret this part of our relationship at all."

"What about it do you regret?"

"Nothing." She shook her head, biting back the admission that was hovering on the edge of her lips. *I regret that I love you, and you will never love me back.*

"I didn't mean to hurt you. If I did…"

"Rodriguez, I'm not going to break," she said. It was like speaking in code. She wondered if he knew she was talking about feelings, not her body. She wondered if he was talking about feelings.

"That's comforting to know," he said, giving her a look that made her feel hot all the way down to her toes.

"You should get ready," she said.

He nodded once and got out of bed, dragging his pants on and walking out of the door. He had to go back to his room so he could find a suit for the press conference. Get showered and presentable.

Carlotta flung herself backward onto the pillows and threw her arm over her face. "I'm such an idiot." Even still, she smiled.

Her phone vibrated from her purse on the floor and she rummaged around until she found it. "Hello?"

"Carlotta, is that you?"

Carlotta sat up again. "Mother? Is everything all right?"

"Yes. No. I don't know if you heard the news about Anna?"

Her brother's ex-intended, the woman he had

ditched for his new fiancée, Allegra. "What about Anna?"

"She's pregnant."

Carlotta's mouth dropped open. "No! She is? What is Alex going to do? Is he still going to marry Allegra or is he…?"

"It's not Alessandro's baby," Zoe said crisply.

"Oh." That truly shocked Carlotta since Anna was about as demure and predictable as they came. Not that that was a bad thing, truly. Carlotta had spent a long time wishing she'd stayed as buttoned up and predictable as sweet Anna. "So… who is…?"

"Leo. Leo Jackson."

Carlotta snorted a laugh in spite of herself. "Those Jacksons." Alex's fiancée's brother had now hooked up with Alex's ex-fiancée. It was like a soap opera. And for the first time, she wasn't the star. And yet, at the moment she didn't really care.

"Well, I hope she's very happy with him."

"How can you say that?" Her mother sniffed. "Now we have no hope! If Alessandro is going to come to his senses—and he must—we needed all the help we could get. But now Anna is…"

"Mother, he doesn't love Anna."

"What does love have to do with anything?"

Carlotta blew out a breath. Her mother, who had never shared a room with her husband, who would never dream of putting her own needs before duty, didn't really shock her with the statement. And a month ago, Carlotta would have agreed. She'd agreed to marry Rodriguez without love after all.

But now, now she knew differently.

"Love has everything to do with it. Everything to do with life."

"You sound strange. Chipper."

"I am. I'm in love." The admission freed her, made her feel light.

"Please tell me it's with Prince Rodriguez or I really will be apoplectic."

"It is, Mama," she said, using the name she hadn't called her mother by in years. "He's wonderful. And I hope Alex and Allegra, and Anna and Leo, are as happy with each other as I am with him. Tell Anna congratulations if you see her."

"I will," her mother said, clearly still not happy, but mollified. "Give Luca a kiss for me."

Carlotta's heart suddenly felt too large for her chest. "I will. Promise."

She was tempted to tell her mother about Rodriguez's father. But she didn't really want to add to the burden.

"*Ciao.*"

"*Ciao*, Mama," she said, hanging up the phone.

Carlotta laughed into the empty room. Her mother had called her. About someone else's scandal. She ranked as a confidante again.

And she didn't care. She was glad to speak to her mother, so happy not to feel the icy reserve anymore. To hear warmth, as much as her mother was capable of.

But she didn't care whether her mother approved of her. Whether her father approved of her. It didn't matter. She was happy. Content. Luca was taken care of. She had balance in her life. She wasn't hiding, wasn't pretending to be someone she just couldn't be. She wasn't forgetting she was a woman, she was being both mother and wife. Well, eventual wife.

And it was *her* life. No one else's.

She didn't know why it had taken so long to figure that out. Why half of the guilt and baggage she carried around with her had to do with other people. The way they saw her. Whether or not *they* were happy with how she was living. For some reason, she'd bought into the idea that she somehow didn't deserve love. That she couldn't have it.

But she did. She could.

She rolled out of bed and went to her closet, hunting for what to wear. It was strange, the kind of freedom being in love with Rodriguez brought.

Her supposed love for Gabriel had felt oppressive, secret and shameful even before she'd found out about his wife. But her love for Rodriguez had come spilling out of her. She hadn't wanted to hide it.

And he needed love. Even if he didn't think he could ever give it back, he needed to feel some.

She couldn't grieve his father. Not knowing what he'd done to Rodriguez. Not knowing how he'd hurt him. How he'd taken a little boy's world and filled it with fear and pain. She couldn't erase the past, but she could help make a better future. For all of them.

That started with supporting him while he gave the hardest speech he would ever have to give.

Carlotta sat in the front row at the press conference, her heart in her throat, as she waited for

Rodriguez to come and stand before them. Before her and the army of press who had assembled themselves at Santa Christobel's palace for the second time that week.

She wished she had some way to relieve the nervous tension in her body, but she didn't want to fidget like a child in a room full of reporters with cameras.

When Rodriguez strode in, she felt everyone in the room draw breath. She did too. He was wearing a black suit, less unruly than normal, but nowhere near respectable.

He moved to the front of the room and held up a hand to silence the chatter. She couldn't take her eyes off him. Off his bearing, the authority he brought with him. Sometime in the past weeks, he'd changed.

Or maybe he hadn't changed. Maybe he was simply free to show the man beneath the layers of protection he had wrapped himself in.

"Thank you all for coming," he said. Then he looked at her, met her gaze. And he didn't look away. "I know it has been in the news already, but I can confirm that my father, King Carlos Anguiano, passed away last night. It is the end of an era for Santa Christobel, and yet I hope we can look to the future. I pledge to rule our country with honor, with integrity and with all the strength I possess."

A murmur of agreement and a sweeping click of camera shutters went through the room.

"And while this is a sad day," Rodriguez continued, "I hope the sadness can be tempered by happy news. I recently learned that I have a son. An heir."

The wave of shocked noise that went through the crowd was short and sharp, and she realized she had gasped too. He didn't mean… Had he fathered a child out of wedlock? Had he just found out? Her heart pounded so fast she was afraid it was going to drain the blood from her head. Afraid she might pass out cold.

Rodriguez waited for everyone to quiet again and she clasped her hands together, squeezing them tight, trying hard to keep her vision from tunneling.

"Luca Santina is my son, with Princess Carlotta Santina, my fiancée, who I know you've already met. He is heir to the throne of Santa Christobel.

And he is now to be called Prince Luca Santina Anguiano. He has my name. My protection."

It was hard to breathe. And it was hot. So hot in this tiny, blasted room. The roar of the press was deafening and she could feel them pressing in closer. Nearer to Rodriguez. To her. She couldn't force her thoughts into order.

Finally, a woman in the back was able to make herself heard over the din. "He is…your son?"

"Yes," Rodriguez said, his voice clipped. "I am Luca's father. I think that's fairly clear based on my previous statements. Are there any other questions?"

The room exploded with noise and Carlotta could only sit and listen to it all happening around her.

"How long have you known?"

"When did your affair with the princess begin?"

"Why didn't you claim him years ago?"

A reporter rushed over to her where she was sitting. "Princess, how did you bring yourself to forgive Prince Rodriguez for leaving you pregnant and alone?"

"I…I didn't need to…"

The man pressed. "Or were you simply not certain if he was the father, or if it was another man?"

She felt her cheeks get hot, her entire body shivering from the inside out. Anger, fear and the intense desire to hide from the intensity of the scrutiny. She hated this. More than almost anything else, she hated being at the center of the frenzy.

A reporter on her other side grabbed her arm, turning her to face him. "Does this mean the only Santina bastard is no longer a bastard?"

There was no air. There was just a teeming throng of suit jackets crushing in on her. Elbows in her face as all the reporters jockeyed for position, as they tried to be the first one to ask the questions, to come up with the most lurid, insulting, vile comments imaginable.

She was pinned in her chair, bodies in front of her and behind her, pressing in. She just wanted to cover her head and hide until they went away, but she couldn't move even that much.

"Everyone move back," she said. The roar of questions was deafening, a sound wall that defeated her.

"Move back." Rodriguez's voice cut through the

noise and the reporters began to move away as he physically pushed them away from her.

His dark eyes were on fire with intensity as he grabbed one man, the first one to put his hands on her, and pulled him back forcibly. The other man started to move back in but Rodriguez took hold of him again, his upper lip curled into a snarl. "I said move back, or you may not ever move again."

This time the reporter didn't challenge him. The entire crowd seemed to shrink beneath Rodriguez's rage, moving away from her. She could breathe again.

"You have all forgotten that Princess Carlotta Santina is royalty. She is my future wife, your future queen. You will all hand in your press badges as you leave. What happens with them later, whether or not you will see them returned, will be decided at my convenience. For now, all you need to know is that Luca is my son. Carlotta is my fiancée. There is no salacious story beneath that. You will give them both the respect they are due."

He was lying. For her. For Luca. He was doing so much more than giving Luca his name. He was claiming him in the most unbreakable, unquestionable way. Taking the birthright from his future biological children and bestowing it onto her son.

Rodriguez walked to where she was sitting and extended his hand. She grasped it and he pulled her to a standing position. She held on to him like a lifeline as they walked out of the press room, her breathing shaky, labored.

She didn't speak, and neither did he, until they were closeted in his office.

Then her entire body started shaking. "I hate this. *Dio*, but I hate this."

Rodriguez stood in front of her, looking at a loss. "What happened was out of line. Beyond the pale. I have half a mind to have some of those men arrested. If I'd had any idea…"

"It's always like that though, isn't it? Maybe not so physical. Maybe not even in person. But the questions and the accusations."

"It's over now, I have declared Luca to be my son. He is my heir. You have no name written in the place designated for a father on his birth certificate, do you?" She shook her head. "Write in mine."

"He's…not your biological son," Carlotta said softly.

"No. But what does that matter, Carlotta? I will protect Luca, I swear it. If anyone ever harmed him…I would end them. And yet my father…my flesh and blood, thought nothing of harming me, keeping me in fear of him. What does blood matter?"

She thought of her own family. She loved them. And she believed they loved her. But it wasn't unconditional. She'd tested the bonds of it, and found they could be broken, and while they had been fixable, they had not healed back the same as they'd been before. He was right. Blood meant nothing.

"It doesn't," she said. She sat in the chair that was positioned by his desk. She felt cold. "I can't stop shaking. I don't know why. It was like this when I was pregnant with Luca. The horrible questions. Constant photos. Headlines. They followed me everywhere. Nothing was mine anymore, not even my own image. They distorted it to make a story. To make money."

Rodriguez looked at Carlotta, at her pale features, her lips chalky white, her eyes dull. He wanted to touch her, to offer her comfort. Something. But he didn't know how. Didn't know what to do, not when he was the one who'd caused her pain.

He shouldn't have had her attend the press conference. He should have anticipated the firestorm. But his decision about Luca had been made suddenly, just before he was preparing to speak.

It had hit him right then, what he had to do. To truly make Luca a part of him. A part of the family. To protect him from rumors, from labels. There would still be rumors, but he had the kind of reputation that would make it easy for his people to believe that he'd fathered a child he hadn't known about.

"I don't know if I can do this," she whispered. "Sometimes I think it was easier when I was in Italy."

Something in his chest broke. Splintered into a million pieces at the soft, sad admission. Still he stood, frozen, unsure of what to do. Unsure if anything he did would ever be enough. If he was the one who was meant to comfort her in this moment.

There was no real way he could ever know. She was here because she'd been manipulated into it. And he hadn't cared. He'd known that she didn't want to marry him, that she was only doing it out of a misguided sense of duty, and he had gone along with it anyway.

Was he truly any better than his father?

She stood, the fatigue etched into her face. "Thank you, Rodriguez. For what you did. I am grateful. I'm sorry about…this. The emotional stuff. I just hate being in the public eye like that. It's not for me. I guess I have to get used to it though, don't I?"

"You should get some rest."

She needed it, after what those animals had done to her. The image of her, surrounded by the crowd of reporters, the gut-tearing rage he'd felt when that man had grabbed her arm, it threatened to choke him.

"Thank you," she said. She turned and walked out of his office, her shoulders stiff, stress evident in every line of her beautiful body.

He simply stood there, suddenly aware that she was being held prisoner. And that he held the keys to her chains. He was forcing her to stay here. Keeping her with him for what? To make himself happier? No matter the cost to her?

His father had done that. Had tried to hold his mother captive with threats, with power.

But unlike his mother, Carlotta wouldn't leave. She wouldn't abandon her son or her duty to slip out of a situation that made her miserable.

The knowledge cut into his chest like a knife, wounding him, making him bleed. It was a new, strange kind of grief. One that flayed him from the inside out. One that made his body like a stranger's.

Carlotta.

She would stay with him forever, ignore her own comfort, her own desire to do what she felt she had to do. And she would grow to hate him for it.

And he would never be able to bear it.

"I'm not sleepy!" Luca protested, the whine in his tone proving that statement to be a lie.

"Yes, you are," Carlotta said.

"Nope," Luca insisted.

"Luca," Rodriguez said, his tone firm. "Don't argue."

Luca's eyes rounded as he looked at Rodriguez. "Okay. I'm sorry."

"I forgive you," Rodriguez said, trying to ignore the crushing weight in his chest.

He'd spent the afternoon thinking of what he must do. What he had to do for Carlotta's happiness. For Luca's.

"Can you carry me?" Luca asked, stretching his arms out to him, the trust in his eyes implicit. Humbling and undeserved.

"Of course," Rodriguez said, lifting him, surprised at the comfort it gave him.

"Rodriguez?"

"What, Luca?" he asked.

"Are you going to be my dad?"

Luca's question cut straight through him. Would he ever be a father to him? Really? Would he be worthy of it? "Yes, Luca," he said. Because he would do all he could. He would be Luca's father, no matter what happened between him and Carlotta. He would see to that.

Luca patted Rodriguez's face. "Good."

Rodriguez's throat felt tight. Too tight. He carried Luca down the hall and put him in his bed, pulling the covers up around him. It was nice, for one moment, to have the kind of domesticity he'd always wondered about. To know it was real.

To know, even as it tore him to pieces, that love was real.

"Can I have Sherbie and Sherbet?"

Rodriguez reached over to Luca's side table and took the stuffed owls from their perch, placing them in Luca's arms. "Anything else?"

"No. Thank you for tucking me in."

"Good night, Luca."

Rodriguez closed the door behind him and walked down the hall to where Carlotta was standing. He couldn't remember the last time he'd felt fear. He felt it now.

"Can we talk?" he asked.

She nodded. "Of course. After today it's probably a good idea."

He wanted to touch her. He knew he shouldn't. If he touched her, he would be lost. He would kiss her if he laid one finger on her silken skin, and once his lips met hers, he would be on fire, inside and out, with the need to join his body to hers.

And no matter how much he wanted to be with her, no matter how badly he wanted to make love, he wouldn't use that to manipulate her. And he wouldn't use it to put a Band-Aid on a situation that was mortally wounded.

"The announcement today changed things," he said, working at detaching emotion from his voice, working at detaching himself from his body. Trying to find that place that was free of everything but the necessary numbness he needed to get through life. To get through this.

"Did it?"

He worked at forcing the words out, his body unwilling to say them. "We no longer have to get married."

She said nothing for a moment, her expression blank, her body frozen. "We don't?"

"No. I have claimed Luca as my biological son. As my heir. That negates the need for us to have any more children." Saying that was like driving a knife into his own stomach. It was the death of elusive dreams he had let himself have for brief, fleeting moments. But he would do it a thousand times to avoid the pain a forced marriage would cause Carlotta.

"And the marriage…"

"The unity came from children. The benefits to the nations from the solid bond that us sharing a child would bring. We share that bond. I…I do think of Luca as my son and I didn't name him as my heir lightly."

"But you don't want to get married?"

Carlotta felt like the world had tilted on its axis and she had remained standing where she was, trying to adjust her perspective in a world that didn't look the same anymore.

Rodriguez's words, words that seemed like they were from another lifetime, came back to her.

I prefer not to marry. But I need an heir.

He'd found a way to get his heir without getting the wife. A way to have what he needed without having to take on the extra baggage a wife would supply.

"What do you…what do you want to do with Luca? With…me?"

"He's my heir and he needs to be in Santa Christobel. If you like, you could live in an apartment on the grounds, or remain in the palace. But somewhere you will both be safe. Be kept away from the public eye."

In the palace? Where she'd have to watch Rodriguez with other women? Where she would have to endure knowing, night after night, that he was down the hall giving them what he had given to her? Something she had thought was special. Different.

What a fool she was.

Because this hadn't been a simple affair. She had given all of herself. Everything, with no reservation. She had stripped off every inhibition, every bit of protection. She had shown Rodriguez who she was. He had shown her who she was. Had taught her things about herself she had never imagined might be true.

He had changed her. And now he was just… leaving her. How could he not want their life together? The one they had planned. How could he have given her the picture of the perfect, domestic family life and then take it back from her? How dare he make her dream again? Make her want and desire and need. And how dare he take those new dreams and tear them into pieces, scattering them in the wind.

"So you have what you want now? And that's… it?"

He looked at her, his eyes flat. Frighteningly dark. This was the man she'd glimpsed beneath the cool, playboy exterior, this was him exposed, stripped of the veneer. He was terrifying, beautiful and utterly heartbreaking.

She wanted to touch him, but she was afraid it might break her. To touch him again and have him reject her.

"I will never have what I want. That's the nature of this life, Carlotta. We live, we try and survive the abuse that is hurled at us, and we either crumble beneath it or we become stronger. There's no light at the end of the tunnel. It's just surviving."

She shook her head. "No. I don't believe that. I want more than that." She swallowed hard, taking a step away from him. "And I'll have that some day. Because I'm not afraid to chase it now. To be me. To grab life with both hands. That's one good thing you did for me, Rodriguez. You showed me that I could be who I am. That I'm happier when I'm not trying to hide. Maybe you should try that. The not-hiding thing."

She turned away from him, because if she looked at him, even for one more second, she would crumble completely. And she couldn't do that. She was going to stay strong. For Luca. For herself. For the new her that Rodriguez had helped her become.

"Where will you go, Carlotta?" he asked, his voice rough.

"Tonight? Just my room. Tomorrow...I don't know."

"And you will take Luca?"

Her stomach tightened. Luca, who loved Rodriguez.

"We will be here, in Santa Christobel. I won't hurt Luca like that." She turned to face him again. "I won't allow you to hurt him."

Rodriguez met her eyes. "I won't."

She believed that. Utterly. Completely. But he would hurt her. He had. He had taken her world and destroyed it. Taken every new and wonderful thing she felt she'd discovered about life and twisted it, handed it back to her a mangled mass of nothing.

She turned again and walked from the room, leaving bits of herself behind. Pieces of herself she didn't think she could ever reclaim.

CHAPTER THIRTEEN

CARLOTTA hadn't left the palace. But she had left him in every way that mattered. She wasn't in his bed. She didn't share meals with him. She hardly spoke to him.

He felt like there was a hole torn through him, raw and bleeding. It made it painful to breathe. He couldn't find solace in retreating from emotions because it had bled into every part of him. It was in his bones.

But he had given her a choice, had told her they didn't have to marry, and she had taken it. It was right. But it was killing him slowly.

To have her so close that all he would have to do was walk down the corridor to be in her arms again, and yet so far that he was certain of her rejection, was torment.

He'd imagined he had known enough pain that he would be dead to it now. He'd been wrong. Laughably wrong.

What he wanted to do was get drunk and forget. Find some artificial happiness and pretend, for a few hours, that it was his reality.

It was what he had done all his life.

But it wasn't enough anymore. It would never be enough again. Carlotta had shown him true happiness. And she had revealed the rest of his life as the shallow counterfeit it was.

Because she had torn the walls around his heart down to the ground. She'd made him love. Had shown him the love a father should have for a son with Luca. Had shown him true love between a man and woman.

He loved her. With every piece of ruined soul, he loved her.

And he had pushed her away because he'd had to. Because if he didn't she would have been unhappy. Because if she stayed he would have to tell her. And she might reject him. It hadn't occurred to him to ask her to stay. He had never believed she would.

He curled his hand into a fist and slammed it down on his desk.

He had never believed he deserved love. Never believed he could have it. He had endless confidence in his skills as a ruler, as a lover. But he had learned to despise who he was deep down. Learned to hate the man that no one could love.

But Carlotta had made him feel differently. Seeing her with Luca had changed the way he saw being a parent. Had made him look at it from the side of the adult, rather than the child. Had made him see that anyone who didn't care for Luca was wrong.

That it was the adult and not the child who was at fault.

He stood from his desk, his heart raging in his chest. Maybe he was wrong. Maybe the hope that was surging through him was for nothing.

But he was going to take a chance. If he laid everything down and was left with nothing, not even a shard of pride, it would be worth it.

Pride he could live without. But he didn't want to live without Carlotta.

"Carlotta. Please let me in."

Carlotta sat up in bed, her chest tightening. She hadn't been sleeping. But she'd done what she'd done every night for the past week. Gone to bed at the same time as Luca, lying there, awake and bleeding emotion until sheer exhaustion forced her into a sleep filled with nightmares.

And she'd imagined Rodriguez coming to her. And in her mind she'd been weak. She'd taken him into her arms with no promises of love, or marriage or anything. Because it seemed like having a piece of him would be better than having nothing of him at all. That was when she had to try to remember that she wanted more. More than what though? More than loving a man with every shred of her being? That was a tall order.

"It's open," she said. Because she wanted to see who would win. Weak Carlotta, or Strong Carlotta. She was rooting for her weaker half.

Rodriguez walked in looking disheveled and more handsome than any man had a right to. More than that, looking at him made her feel sated and starving at the same time. She'd been trying not to look at him if they happened to pass each other. And it was pretty easy to avoid someone in a gigantic palace.

He exhaled and crossed the room in two easy strides, sitting on the bed. She wasn't sure who moved first, only that one moment she was determined to be resolute, and the next she was kissing him. Kissing him like she was starving for him, her fingernails digging into his shoulders, tears streaming down her face.

When they parted, he rested his forehead against hers, his breathing labored. "I am a fool, Carlotta."

"I'm listening," she said.

"You don't have to be my wife. I told you that a few days ago. But I shouldn't have left it there. I should have finished with a question."

"What question?"

"Will you marry me? Because you want to. Because I love you. Not because it's your duty, or because you want Luca to have my name. All of that is covered, and marrying me won't give it to you again. But it will make me the happiest man on earth."

She wiped tears from her cheeks with shaking hands. "What did you just say?"

"I asked you to marry me."

"The other part."

"That I love you?"

"Yes. Say it again."

"I love you, Carlotta. I should have told you this before, but I was too afraid. I was numb for so long, and you brought feeling back. Color. Light.

I didn't want to admit how much I needed it. You showed me what life really was, and I didn't think I could live if I lost it. If I confessed it and you didn't feel the same. Somehow, I thought if I could just keep it all inside, I wouldn't have to face it. But I can't deny it. I love you, Carlotta Santina. No woman has ever had my heart. But you do. You have my heart, my mind. My body and my soul."

He cupped her face with his hands. "I cannot deny it. I don't want to. You…you have cast the fear from me with your love. There is no room for it now. I am filled. I am complete."

"I love you too," she said. "I love you so much."

He pulled her to him again, holding her in his arms, just holding her. His breathing ragged, his heartbeat steady and hard against her cheek. "You have no idea how badly I needed to hear that. How much I need your love. I do. I need it. I spent my whole life searching for some kind of happiness, for family. I finally have it. You gave it to me."

"And you gave me freedom. I'm not afraid of myself. Of passion. You accept me as who I am. And you've helped me do the same."

"That's love, Carlotta," he said, as though he was suddenly the expert. "Love has no conditions.

No bounds. I didn't realize that until I met you. Thank you," he said, his voice rough. "Thank you for finding me. I was buried underneath a facade I hated. You found me."

Tears slid down her face, matching his. "I have loved every piece of you, Rodriguez. The man you showed the world, the father you are to our son, the man you are just for me. And I always will."

Rodriguez didn't bother to fight the emotion that was rushing through him, emotion he had kept shut off for so long. Emotion unlocked by Carlotta. By her love.

"I believe you."

"Good, because I'll always tell you the truth," she said.

"I know."

"I love you. And I want to marry you. Not to atone for anything, but because with you I'm free. With you I finally know who I am."

"That's good, Carlotta," he said, taking her face in his hands, wiping her tears away. "Because you are exactly who I needed."

EPILOGUE

"WE'RE outnumbered." Rodriguez surveyed the lawn, crowded with toys and climbing structures, and children. Four of them, running everywhere.

Luca was chasing the three smaller children and they were shrieking with glee.

"Yes, we are," Carlotta said, a smile lighting up her beautiful face. Seven years on and Rodriguez didn't think he would ever get used to her beauty. He was struck by it every time he looked at her.

Elizabetta, their youngest daughter, ran over to the slide and took two stuffed owls from the end.

"Those owls have seen better days," he said wryly.

"It's true, but they've been well loved by all."

Rodriguez turned to his wife, his heart, his soul. "Have I told you today that I love you?"

Her lips curved up into a smile. "You told me pretty emphatically this morning right after you…"

"I mean, have I told you since we got out of bed?"

"Once at breakfast. Then again during lunch. I think again when you passed me in the hall."

"Then I should tell you again. I love you, Carlotta Anguiano."

"And I love you too, more today than yesterday."

Rodriguez pulled her close, holding her against his chest as they watched their children play. For a man who had worked so hard, for so long, chasing happiness, it was a wonderful thing to simply rest in it.

* * * * *